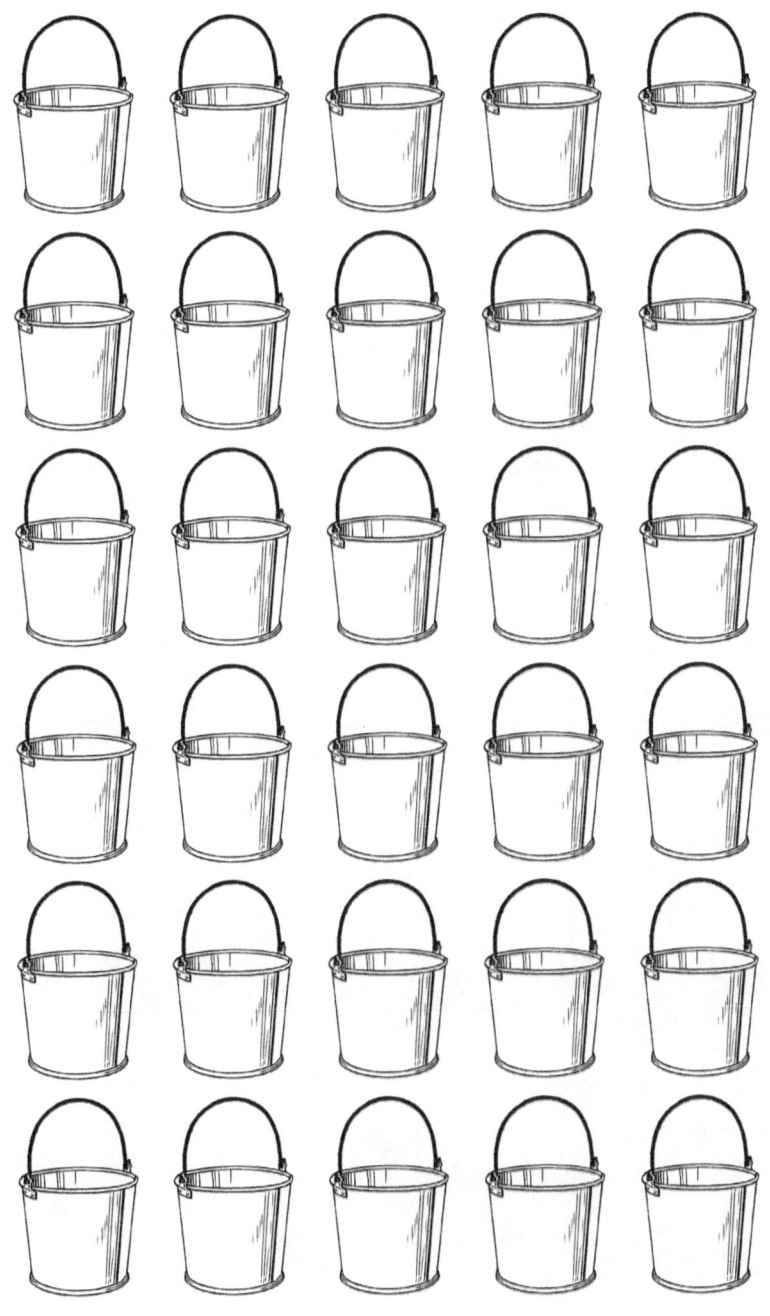

Pure Slush Books

2014

June

Vol. 6

a Pure Slush book

Pure
Slush

2014 June Vol. 6 is edited by Matt Potter and
published by Pure Slush, April 2014.

ISBN: 978-1-925101-49-2

You can find *Pure Slush* at http://pureslush.webs.com

Copies of all *Pure Slush* publications can be bought
at http://pureslush.webs.com/store.htm

All queries re *Pure Slush* can be made
via email to edpureslush@live.com.au

A note on differences in punctuation and spelling

Pure Slush proudly features (both online and in print) writers from all over the English-speaking world. Some speak and write English as their first language, while for others, it's their second or third or even fourth language. Naturally, across all versions of English, there are differences in punctuation and spelling, and even in meaning. These differences are reflected in the stories *Pure Slush* publishes, and it accounts for any differences in punctuation, spelling and meaning found within these pages.

stories by

Guilie Castillo-Oriard

James Claffey

Townsend Walker

Gwendolyn Joyce Mintz

Derek Osborne

Stephen V. Ramey

Gloria Garfunkel

Gay Degani

John Wentworth Chapin

Sally-Anne Macomber

Lynn Beighley

Mandy Nicol

Andrew Stancek

Margaret Bingel

Rachel Ambrose

Darryl Price

Gill Hoffs

Teresa Burns Gunther

Susan Tepper

Matt Potter

Jessica McHugh

Gary Percesepe

Shane Simmons

Nathaniel Tower

Michelle Elvy

Kimberlee Smith

Len Kuntz

Vanessa Weibler Paris

Michael Webb

Joanne Jagoda

for

Rebecca Chekouras

for fighting

the good fight

When the Sunset

by Guilie Castillo-Oriard

The sunset has turned the Caribbean sky into the fire-streaked excess one associates with Photoshop zealots. Luis Villalobos, on a towel by the surf, is thinking about leaving. It's been impossible to get Pélagie alone all afternoon. She's doing it on purpose; she just doesn't give a damn, and Luis is a fool for thinking one more try, after so many, will make any difference.

Al is romping with the other dogs, tearing up gusts of sand at the far end of the cove. Chases, gets chased, chases again. Staccato growls – part of the game, Pélagie said – reach Luis intermittently, depending on the wind. His dog is happy. Luis can sit here a while longer, for Al if not for Ehrlich Fiduciary, or for Pélagie Solak, and ponder his defeat.

He hinged, stupidly, his whole career at Ehrlich on this one corporate structure, this one woman.

He doesn't see Pélagie until she touches a cold beer to the sunburned patch of skin above his shirt collar. "I'm glad you brought Al." She hands him the beer, clinks her own against it in a token toast.

He means to take just a sip – he doesn't need more beer, he has to drive that potholed road back to what passes for civilization on this island – but it tastes so good

15

he downs half in three gulps. "I didn't expect him to make friends so fast."

"They just need time." She bends her willowy body and sits cross-legged on his towel. Her knee bumps his thigh and he moves to make more room. "Sorry," she says, edges onto the sand.

"No, it's – please, sit on the towel."

She pins him in place with those disturbingly clear green eyes that nothing can wriggle away from. "I'm all sandy anyway."

This woman makes Luis feel profane. Around her, anything he says, everything about him, feels like unadulterated crudeness. A tenor pulling out his dick mid-*Turandot*.

"I make you nervous, don't I?"

Away from her gaze – she's looking at the dogs – he's brave enough to chuckle. "Not nervous, no."

"I'm not much good around people."

Luis glances over her shoulder at the crowd gathered around the bonfire. He just met them earlier today, hasn't traded more than a fistful of words with them, but it was enough to know they came – some with dogs, some without and apologetic for it – because Pélagie is here. "Could've fooled me."

She follows his gaze. "Because of them?"

"Seems like a nice group of friends."

"Groupies, really." She smiles, perhaps to take off some of the sting. "They like being associated with me because of who I am, not because of me."

Platitudes line up, ready to deploy, but then she says, "Know what I mean?" It's that phrase people tack onto the end of an awkward statement; it's not a real question. But the hell of it is Luis *does* know. He's done it, basked in others' glow – hotshot investment managers, celebrity clients – as if their magic might rub off on him, give him a glow of his own for others to bask in. And how good he felt, how vindicated, when it did. He wants to tell Pélagie there's nothing wrong with an entourage; it's proof of one's worth to the world. But he's afraid it might sound defensive. "They seem to like you," he says instead.

"They don't know me. They think they do, enough even to judge. But they don't know shit."

Her bitterness startles him. Then it occurs to him he might fit into this category. "Do you think I'm judging?"

She touches the beer to her lips, hesitates before taking a hasty sip. "Maybe. A little."

"Because of the affidavit?"

She's digging her bare foot into the sand. It's a beautiful foot, weightless and unadorned like the rest of her. "You think I'm wrong, you're right. That's a judgment."

"I don't mean it to be. I don't – I want to understand, but –"

"And I've explained. You just don't listen."

"No, I do." He collects himself, wants to avoid sounding belligerent. "You don't want to be a party to tax evasion. Neither does Ehrlich Fiduciary, Pélagie. That's not what we do. That's not what your structure is for."

"It's artificial." She flexes her toes and sand trickles between them, catches on ridges of skin. "I run a dog rescue group, Luis. I don't need companies in the British Virgin Islands or Barbados. Or New Zealand."

"It's because of the treaties. They allow tax deferral –"

"Listen to you." She chuckles, smooths the edge of the towel. "Treaties. Tax deferral. I talk to you for five minutes and I start feeling like I need a tailored suit and a briefcase."

"And you hate boardrooms, I know. But –" Luis lowers his voice. "The fact remains, Pélagie, you're a woman of substantial wealth. It's my job to –"

"I don't want it." She turns those eyes on him, full blast. "Okay? That substantial wealth, as you call it, means nothing but – obligation. And damned if I'll skirt that obligation, too."

"I'm lost. What – ?"

But she just keeps going. "The dogs balance it out. They make it – good. The money can do good, like this. See?"

There's a pleading in the last word that stops him from arguing. Of course he could keep arguing, even now that he doesn't understand what she's talking about – obligation? to whom? – because what good is a lawyer who can't debate three sides of an issue, can't push an advantage when he sees one? She could do so much more with the money that will otherwise go to the government in taxes. Save more dogs, if that's what she wants to do. But the conversation seems to have sidestepped into emotion he has no context for.

He should've let this go long ago. Ignored it back in April, like Milena wanted; processed the resignations last month, like Milena instructed. Milena was, as she always is, right. He's made this personal, but it isn't until now, when it's all about to end, that he realizes – admits – how personal.

It doesn't matter. It's over. "We'll file the resignation documents tomorrow."

Pélagie glances at him. "Thank you."

"Don't thank me. The whole structure will fall apart."

But – and this is not really surprising anymore, although it's still frustrating – she doesn't look worried. "Saves me the trouble of dissolving it."

"That's not how it works." But he says no more – really, what good would it do at this point? Her disdain, for him and for the logic that rules his life, already crusts every exchange. He would've anyway, though, except that Al chooses that moment to come check up on his human. He barrels onto Luis, all drool and wet, sandy paws. All unreserved worship and joy, too, which is why Luis smiles instead of grimacing and doesn't even wipe away the gobs of saliva – it could be ocean water – on his arm. He does, however, apologize for the sand sprayed in Pélagie's direction. "He thinks he's a Chihuahua. Don't you, guy? Hey, are you thirsty? Want some water, Al?"

"I set some out for them, too." Pélagie rubs the dog's chest, who looks for all the world like he's never experienced anything so delicious, the turncoat, as Luis pours from a thermos into the travel bowl.

Al splashes out double what he drinks, gets petted, patted, and scratched, before rejoining – not without a vigorous shake devised so that equal amounts of water and sand land on both humans – the other dogs.

Luis sputters, spits sand. Pélagie laughs, wipes at her face with a hand that has more dog hair, finally peels off her tank top. "I'm going to rinse off."

It takes Luis only a minute to take off shirt and shorts to follow her into the water, but in that minute memories of New Year's Eve crowd him – the walk on the beach with Milena, the fateful soak in the darkness, the drunken sex. Consequences. When he does wade in, he keeps a careful distance. Not that Pélagie would ever – hell, she doesn't even *like* him.

He lets the moment, the memories, dissolve. Then he says, in what might be a Guinness Record for Most Awkward Change of Subject: "You never told me how you got involved in dog rescuing."

"You mean how I became the crazy dog lady?" She grins, blows at the surface so the water ripples. "Don't apologize. Living with eighteen dogs qualifies me, I think. I'm even proud of it, which makes it so much more dysfunctional." He laughs, and she looks at him. The smoldering sunset lights her face like sun through stained glass. "You really want to know?"

"I do."

"It's a long story. And corny. Maudlin."

"I like maudlin." A lie, but it sounds convincing. Good lawyer, good boy. Or maybe it's not a lie. Because Luis is discovering he's fallen in love.

19

La Ronde / Gloria and Serge

by Townsend Walker

Serge, personal trainer Serge, walks up the path to 151 Carmelina in Brentwood, Gloria and Myron's place. Yes, Myron has returned to Gloria; rather, she has allowed him back into her life. Actually, she pretty much begged him to come back home. Had to. Who doesn't want to be the wife of the guy whose film, *The Naked Corpse*, was picked up by Paramount? With Marty signing on to direct, meaning Bobby, Sean, Leo and Jules will star. (That's Scorcese, De Niro, Penn, De Caprio and Roberts.) Mistress back in Newark be damned.

Gloria's Great Dane, Zeus, bounds from the bushes, leaps up on Serge: Tom Cruise tall, muscled like Sly Stallone, with a shock of bright blonde hair atop a preternaturally tanned face. Zeus crowds his muzzle into Serge's face. The dog's front legs are weighing on his shoulders. One hundred and fifty pounds of dog flesh. Zeus has got to be thinking: *Oh what fun, someone to play with.* Serge leans back and smacks the dog across the nose.

"Get off me, vile creature, go chew bone."

Zeus, oblivious, laps Serge's face with his wide slobbery tongue. Serge kicks the dog's hind leg, hard; the dog yelps. Gloria, in her white workout clothes, Swarovskis sprinkled around the neckline, comes out on the porch.

"Don't you so like to be greeted by this friendly puppy? Good dog Zeusie, making Sergie so welcome."

"Ach, yes, nice dog, wish I had one, my own."

Serge ruffles the dog's head tenderly.

"Okay Zeus, down now, Serge and Mommy have to get to work."

Gloria and Serge hug and loud air kisses float through the garden.

"So Myron back? I hear from friend."

"Yes, the little lamb has become a lion, but we have an agreement now that I'll be on location with him when shooting starts."

"Gloria, must start routine."

"God, what a taskmaster you've become. I'd swear you were German, not Russian."

"We more fierce than Germans. We win, they lose."

"Not the way I heard it," she says. "My history professor in college said General Winter won it for you."

"Who General Winter? We no have a General Winter."

"The weather, you big doofus. The cold and snow killed the Nazis, not the Soviets."

"Not what I taught. Brave Soviet troops sacrifice for motherland."

"Whatever," Gloria shrugs.

They walk through the house to the sun porch Gloria has outfitted as her exercise studio. Had a shower put in so after a workout she doesn't have to walk through the rest of the house perspiring. Porch done in shades of pink ranging from cherry blossom to magenta, including the weights, yoga mat, and exercycle. The Monday session starts with a high-energy routine mixing jumping jacks, skipping rope and running in place to rid the body of the toxins built up during the weekend (alcohol and just the "tiniest" bit of coke). Followed by weights, tantric stretches and a massage. This is Gloria's favorite part. Serge has very good hands. She's had dreams about him, but unfortunately for her, he dreams only of Jimmy.

"Lower there, Serge, yes, oh yes, that's the place."

"Tell about movie. Role for Serge?"

"I don't know, I'll ask if they need any Russian muscle men."

"I not only muscle. Study to act. Have Equity card from Jimmy. And, who do your workout on location?"

There is no way Myron would give Serge a role. To change the subject she talks about Myron bumping into some guy back East who tells him about this contract a woman has put out on her husband. He beats her up. On top of that, he loses the kids when he takes them to the park. Twice they ended up calling the cops to find the seven and ten year old. Seems the guy gets distracted, or off doing something else, who knows.

"She doesn't want a divorce, she wants a death." That's Gloria's take.

She turns over on the massage table so her face is cosseted in the headrest.

"What he like?"

Gloria's description comes out a bit muffled.

Serge repeats: "Tell me if I understand. Franklin Lincoln Cabot Three. He called Frank. Work at Goldman Sachs on West Street, Manhattan. Six foot three, 250 pounds, pasty like dough face, curly black hair with silver, big nose like bird, Brooks suits, loafers with tassels. And Hermes ties. Prada (I know Prada, Jimmy wear Prada, I want to wear Prada) Aviators, blue tint. He wear even in rain."

Gloria turns her face up to Serge. "Why do you care about this? You got some friends that have guns?"

"How much lady in New York pay?"

"Myron wasn't sure, but reckoned around fifty big ones, maybe more. She seemed desperate."

"So when lady talk to Myron?"

Serge can be thick sometimes, Gloria's thinking. "Myron never talked to the lady, he got the story from someone who got it from someone."

"So how you know he not dead now?"

"Call him up. If he answers, he's not dead."

"You have name lady want husband dead?"

Gloria slips off the massage table and wraps herself in a cerise pink robe. "Serge, don't you have another appointment?"

In the afternoon Serge calls Gloria. "Cannot find name in phone book."

"What name?"

"Name of lady pays for murder husband."

Gloria throws the phone across the room, quickly retrieves it.

"What that noise? Hurt ear."

"Serge sweetheart, for the very last time, I will never speak to you if you bring this up again. I told you because I thought you'd have a laugh. Forget it. Goodbye."

Sinking

by Derek Osborne

Well the sun is slowly sinking down …

Max and Rebecca are sitting in the cockpit, snuggled under the big, patchwork quilt they stole off the bunk. It's been warm and sunny all day but now it's grown chilly, a northeast breeze coming in off the ocean, the front will be here by morning. In early June it's always a toss-up on Nantucket. Don't like the weather? Wait a minute.

Rebecca is drinking hot chocolate after eating a roast beef sandwich, two avocadoes and half a pack of Oreos. It's what she wanted. Max learned long ago not to quibble with the desires of a pregnant woman. She's beginning to show. She has that glow all women have by their third month.

"And my ass hurts enough as it is."

She's been complaining all day, seems he can't do anything right, seems he cannot do one damn thing – nothing – he can't even disappear properly. He just smiles when she complains, which ticks her off even more.

"You forget, I've been through this before," he says.

"Well I haven't."

A minute later she's crying and apologizing for being a bitch.

The food seems to help. They're listening to the impromptu band the crew put together. It's becoming a regular Tuesday affair. Eddie brings the boat in around seven and ties alongside the peer. Every musician on the island shows up. They even come out on the ferry from Hyannis. Max puts them up for the night if they can't find (or afford) a bed onshore. In the morning the deck is a sea of sleeping bags, as if the boat, too, has her own patchwork quilt.

At first the Dock Master complained about the concerts so Anja had a little chat with the Chamber of Commerce. In her own gentle way (no one expects The Spanish Inquisition) she explained how good the Tuesday night jams were for business, how the scene lent a certain cachet which, quite frankly, they had blown with all their condominium management, planned events and homogenized building codes. A weathered gray shingle is a weathered gray shingle is a weathered gray shingle. *Gadabout,* in Anja's opinion, is the only surprise left on the island, and word is getting round on the mainland the old Nantucket, the one people love and remember, is back for the season. She even wrangled full artistic direction over what music they'll play. When Anja suggests they have a donation basket for the island's Nature Foundation, The Chamber buys in, hook, line and sinker. Sometimes Jazz, sometimes Rock, last week it was first chair from The Boston Pops – Mozart floating over the harbor – putting the Dock Master squarely in their corner. Fait accompli. Tonight it's Folk Rock.

and you can sing this song ...

"You warm enough?" Max says.
"Yes, I'm fine. Eddie makes a mean cocoa."
They haven't stopped talking since that day last month when Max was still in the hospital. Neither one needed

explanation; Rebecca had her own confession. If you have ever capsized a large boat you know it doesn't happen all at once, it takes time – what seems like a very long time – and in that first rush of panic, knowing you've gone too far, and that slow, deliberate bend to the other side, the confusion of gravity, the water and the rigging, how surprising the power of adrenaline, the will to get out, get out and swim for your life. Waiting for Rebecca to say something after telling her the hospital room number was like that, and when she did answer, when she broke that long, terrible silence, "I'm pregnant," all Max could do was surrender, there would be no escape.

... you can stay as long as you like.

"Have I ever said how good you smell?"
"Please don't start that again."
He's kissing her chocolate mustache. Eddie put whipped cream in the cocoa. It's strange to think it's already been three months. They got pregnant that very first night back in March. She carries it well. It's easy enough to hide and they've been trying to figure out when to go public. CBS intends to announce she is leaving *Miami Blue* at the end of the month. They're letting her do her own press (with a little input from legal). It will be a paparazzi stampede for a month and there will be no way to hide the pregnancy, or Max for that matter, and sooner or later some enterprising reporter will find out about his cancer and then they will have all of that to deal with, tabloid hell. Times like these, where they can simply be alone with friends, will cease to exist.
"Have you thought about a name?" Rebecca says.
They went for an ultrasound this morning. The island's clinic has the equipment but the technician is only there Tuesdays. It's a boy. They wanted to know in case ... just in case. "Finally," Max said when the technician pointed out

the penis. Everything looks fine. The date will be early November. "Scorpio, like me," Rebecca said when they left.

"Of course," Max says now.

"What's that supposed to mean?"

"I've always been a sucker for Scorpio women."

"You should have warned me you were ..."

Max fills in the sentence. "Cancer?"

The simplest of words trigger so many others. Their days are filled with innuendo, embarrassed smiles, Max remembers how it was with Maggie, how the dynamic shifts, the cared-about becomes the care-taker. Add Rebecca's pregnancy.

"It will play well on HBO," she says.

"When did you know?" he says, wanting to change the subject. He's pulled the quilt even higher, there's plenty of room; they're in a kind of cocoon. The band has finished the song, people applauding, not only onboard but also the crowd on the dock. Others have come in their dinghies and rafted at *Gadabout's* stern. There's a directness between Max and Rebecca now, no subject taboo, no room for fears or petty jealousies. "You looked at me," he says. "You were down in the cockpit working out blocking and you looked at me."

"You were up by the bow," she says.

The applause dies down, the band discussing what to play next.

"And then you crashed the boat," she whispers.

"Almost crashed ..."

"*Almost* crashed ..."

"How many girls get to say that?"

The sun is nearly gone, it's warm beneath the quilt, the lights of the village coming on one by one, the floods on the white steeple rising over the hill, soft orange lamps at the docks and gray waterfront.

"A couple days into the shoot one of the make-up guys said you were pretty hot for an older man and I defended you."

This makes him smile.

"And then you almost crashed the boat."

"And you laughed and I fell in love."

The band is beginning another song.

Why must every generation think their folks are square?

"I like this song," Max says, touching his forehead to hers. He reaches under the bulky wool sweater and lifts her t-shirt, placing the flat of one hand on her belly and the other on the small of her back. His hands are warm. The two of them settle in, safe there beneath the cover, he can smell her hair and feel her breathing.

"Maximus Miguel Caamano Vasquez-Perkins," she says.

"Oh God, I've gotta change my name."

"I like your name."

"Perkins?"

"It's so … American."

And still he'll stick his fingers in the fan.

Night is settling in. The sky is a mix of clouds and stars and a quarter moon. There's the deepening chill but for now it's okay; for now they are fine. Tomorrow they'll go looking for a house on the island, some place back from the road, room for both families. Rebecca's inviting her mother and brothers. The house is Pam's idea and his daughters agree (they think the boat is getting awkward) but it's also a way to provide a fortress for the upcoming battle. They can guard the narrow drives, there's no getting through the dense growth on the island or landing a boat in the marsh, and choppers cost a grand an hour. Anja says TV Drama

Show Stars don't rate a chopper. Max squeezes Rebecca's belly, feeling the weight she's gained. He doesn't know the guy who is playing guitar but he's good, a set musician out of Boston. He pulls her close.

The pain and fear come at odd times, the way Max imagines it must be for vets suffering flashbacks. The attacks stab at different parts of his body. He imagines the boat heeling hard, the wind shrieking up in the rigging, sails torn, the deck a confusion of lines and equipment after a rogue wave. He's watching the life-raft fly off into the night. He burrows down beneath the quilt and places his cheek on Rebecca's belly, his arms around, bracing the sound of splintering masts and whip-lashed cables. The waves come huge and mountainous. He grits his teeth, stifles the urge to moan. They'll survive, they always have, but each time the day draws nearer. He squeezes her tight.

"Darling, I can see the moon," Becca says, lifting his face in her hands, "Come here with me and watch the stars."

Depression

by Gloria Garfunkel

Depressive Crash Ralph here. The worst depressions come after the highest manias. I contemplate all day different ways to kill myself: Drowning. Overdoses. Hanging. Shooting. Stabbing. Crashing my car. Jumping from the Mystic River Bridge. (That always gets *Boston Globe* headlines, not that I'm looking for attention.) They all have their downsides. I favor painless but dread the possibility of lifelong coma. The higher my mania gets, the harder I fall. Every time. I'm going to get my psychiatrist to get me a medical leave for the month. I can't keep any of my resolutions. I am a completely inconsistent loser with an empty brain. I don't even meet the most basic Quality Assurance principles in living my life. Maybe I should hand my life over to Scientology. That would be worse than suicide.

Meanwhile Serena is taking total advantage of my helpless situation at work, tracking all my errors and omissions, reporting them to Stan who then calls me into his office to lecture me for half-an-hour jumping on his chair, not a good use of Quality Assurance time I restrain myself from saying aloud but note to put in my report.

When I get home bedraggled and contemplating a car accident, Chloe is gentle and encouraging and makes me soup and tea. I love her.

Ebony

by John Wentworth Chapin

They stand on Esther's stoop, Charles on the top step, Marla two behind him. Charles is aware, as usual, of Esther's neighbors monitoring him. He knocks again, his eyelid twitching and stomach grinding. They wait.

"Maybe she's napping," Marla says. Charles knows this isn't the case; one of Esther's agonies is that she can't relax enough to sleep. Or is this also a lie? Charles doesn't know what is true and what isn't.

He hasn't seen Esther for a month. Charles was surprised yesterday when he got a voicemail from her asking him to come today. Things are different with her now. After months of sympathy – she would never walk again, she was distraught about killing that woman and those boys, she was hounded by lawsuits from the families – sympathy which culminated in his promise to help her plan her own suicide, he discovered she'd been lying to him.

He told his friend Stephanie about it. She saw Esther's suicide plan as a cry for help, and the dishonesty made it obvious. Charles didn't know what to think; he was lost. Stephanie encouraged him to help Esther to regain the will to live. *You can't be angry. You have to help her.* She insisted.

31

So he called the three families of the accident victims, hoping they might reconsider their lawsuits in the wake of her tremendous grief. But his calls were met with confusion. There were no lawsuits.

Charles was dumbfounded. Lie after lie ... but the coup de grâce was remembering that, of course, Esther had lied from the very start. She'd told the doctors and police that she remembered nothing of the accident when, in fact, she remembered every last detail and was haunted by it.

Or so she said. He trusted nothing now.

Into the picture comes Marla. Her sister was killed in the accident. Like the rest of the victim's families, she believes that some sort of neurological blackout led to Esther driving up onto the sidewalk and taking out three people at 40 miles an hour. When Charles explained that Esther was stricken with suicidal guilt and irrational fear about non-existent lawsuits, Marla agreed to make the visit, to reassure poor Esther that no one blamed her for anything. "The last thing any of us needs right now is another death," she said.

Now she's standing in his shadow on Esther's stoop, enormous black purse on her shoulder held carefully, as though someone might at any moment grab it. When Esther doesn't answer her door after the third knock, Charles puts his face to the crack in the door and calls out her name. No response. And then he realizes that he doesn't expect one. She's in there, but she's not asleep. Or awake.

He wishes he was far away from here.

Charles, this is Esther. Esther Pinkney. If you could be so kind and return my call when you get the chance, I'd be much obliged. I was hoping you'd pay me a visit soon to continue our research.

He'd called her back immediately, angry that she'd lied to him.

"I didn't think you'd come unless you felt sorry for me," she said, simply.

"I never came over because I pitied you!" he shouted. "I came because – we had a project together. We *trusted* each other."

"We still have a project, Charles."

"But you lied to me! I was there because I *wanted* to be there, and after the accident … the only person I *haven't* felt crazy around was you."

"It's a shame I didn't realize that," she answered.

"And now you've taken that away from me, too," he bawled, and as he felt his throat constrict with a surprising surge of emotion, he clicked the phone off. What did she care?

After that, she called him every few days, hanging up without leaving a message when he didn't answer. Each time, he thought he might take the call, that he was ready; each time he screened it. Finally, she left him a message, the day before.

Charles, this is Esther. Esther Pinkney. You made me a promise, and unless I hear otherwise from you, I assume you intend to keep it. I'd be obliged if you could stop by tomorrow after work.

The front door is unlocked, and as Charles opens it, he and Marla are slammed by a foul, eggy stench.

"Oh, God! What is that?" Marla shrieks, her hand instinctively shielding her nose and eyes.

Charles guesses it's toilet bowl cleaner mixed with pesticide, a popular and foolproof recipe for hydrogen sulfide gas. The websites say it will kill a person in five minutes. Esther had decided against it, concerned about police or neighbors who would try to help and expose themselves to the lethal gas. The Internet is filled with stories about first responders succumbing to the gas.

He pulls Marla by the arm, and they stumble down the stoop away from the house. She sputters in surprised confusion. "Run – that's poison gas!" Charles yells.

Marla scrambles to join Charles running away from the foul odor. "How do you know?" she yells at him.

"We had – she had talked about suicide," Charles stammers. On the sidewalk now, he tries to pull himself together, too wired now to think clearly. Esther's neighbors look at Charles and Marla with alarm, and the man next door walks across Esther's yard to her front door.

"Don't go in there!" Marla screams at him as she pulls her phone from her giant black purse. "It's poison." She dials 911 and puts a finger in her ear to block out the street noise.

"I can't just leave her in there," the man says.

"It's hydrogen sulfide – poison gas. She's already dead, probably. We – we can't go in." Charles tries to say more but can't. He's frozen.

"Now how do *you* know what's going on in there?" the man says.

Marla is shouting into her phone, explaining the situation.

The man's face changes, his eyebrows knitting. "I've seen you over here before. Just what are you up to with Miss Esther?"

Police, fire trucks, ambulance, news vans, HAZMAT. They clear a perimeter around Esther's house, and Charles watches as men wheel a covered stretcher, which disappears in an ambulance without sirens.

He hears Marla talking rapid-fire to the police the whole time, to the firefighters, the EMTs, to anyone who will listen. Marla won't make eye contact with Charles. She implies, loudly, that he is responsible, and Esther's neighbor seems to agree, stands beside her, nodding and frowning. Charles imagines what happens next: police descend on his apartment, take his computer, search his hard drive, and find his Google history:

> drugs that cause heart attacks
> household poisons
> how to make hydrogen sulfide gas
> carbon monoxide poisoning

A detective approaches Charles, introducing herself, and asks if she can have a moment of his time.

"Of course," Charles whispers.

"Can you tell me what's happened here?"

Charles fears the worst, but he reminds himself he has nothing to hide.

He tells the whole story; at first, he needs prodding from the detective, but soon it all spills out. He couldn't stop talking if he tried. It's a confusing story; the detective wants to know about now, maybe about the past 24 hours, but Charles is back six months ago with the car accident, the odd friendship, the Internet research, the suicide request, the lies. The non-existent lawsuits, the hydrogen sulfide recipe, the phone calls. It makes his own head spin, but the detective listens, nodding and taking notes. Charles has no idea what the detective thinks.

Charles lays out his final defense: "She called me to ask me to come over today. She left me a voicemail."

The detective makes a few notes on a little pad, nodding to herself.

"Oh, shit," Charles says. Intuition stops him cold.

The detective looks up, waiting. "What," she prompts.

35

Charles' mouth is dry as charcoal. "She knew I'd be the first one on the scene. She tried to take me with her." When he says it, he knows it's true.

Infamy

by Lynn Beighley

My cell phone rings and I flinch. Pollock jumps off the bed. I let it ring, even though it's a new unlisted number and only a few people know it.

I reach over to the nightstand and pour another glass of wine, dripping a little on the pink blanket. Wine stains can only improve it. It's been on this bed since I was 12. I consider getting up and ripping down the lacy white canopy over my head, but decide it's too much trouble.

I take a big swig of wine to wash down my vitamin D. A couple weeks ago I read that when you can't go outside, it's a good idea to take D. And wine is supposed to be healthy too, right? So I'm being healthy. I'm being healthy at 11 AM.

I reach across the bed and grab my laptop where I left it last night. Time for me to read the latest about my obsession. Which is me. Or rather news about me, conjectures about where I've gone, comments from all over this great country praising or damning me.

There's not much about me today. No news, no new conjectures. Just a few nasty comments. I sip my wine and check my email. I've got nothing else to do, no job, no reality tv wedding to plan.

My dad knocks on the door. "Come in," I say. He comes in and sits on the edge of the bed.

"Jenn, sweetie, you really need to get up," he says. "And," he sniffs, "take a shower."

"No thanks," I say.

"You can't go on like this," he says.

"I think I can. I see no reason why I can't go on like this."

"Well, if that's how you feel, then you won't mind if the TV folks film you in bed."

I am shocked, but I'm a woman with great self-control. I choose my words carefully.

"What the fuck are you talking about?!"

"You need the money, and they're paying a lot, Jenn. A whole lot. They want you back on the show. Doing whatever you want. You can scream at Bill, whatever. They need you."

I hear a noise outside the door, and see the business end of a film camera, pointed at me.

Kamikaze

by Andrew Stancek

The General gnashes his teeth and a scrap of egg yolk falls from his shaking fork onto his crisp day uniform. Three times a week he meets Dewhurst for a working breakfast, with Dewhurst sipping coffee and buttering toast he'll never eat while the General devours the lumberjack special.

"Damn it, Dewhurst. Millions. Tens of millions we've spent and we're still in a black hole. The best minds working for us and all they've accomplished are pathetic little hops. Hops. We can pretend to be pleased, pretend we're making wonderful progress but we have no flights. They're hops. Bloody Maharishi in the seventies had his disciples hopping, too, without our kind of money and our research team. And here we are, ten years of pouring money down the drain and we're not a nanometer further than he was."

The General slurps orange juice, bangs the glass, refills from the pitcher next to his elbow, overfills, oblivious to the puddle. "And a kid, a snivelly wide-eyed nobody, named Adam, Adam goddamn it, figures it out on his own? And won't tell us how it's done? Won't take our money? If we can't buy him, Dewhurst, other methods will be deployed. You have to break eggs to make an omelet, you know that."

He reaches for the ketchup, pours half the bottle over his home fries. "I want the pathetic kid singing like a canary, telling us, teaching us, leading a fucking parade, dying to share everything he knows. Hooked up to heart monitors and brain wave readers, to every piece of machinery known to science, he'll warble. And if he doesn't, we'll see how he likes a pat on the head and a few jolts of 220 volts into his nipples and penis. We'll watch the pretty blue eyes tremble. We'll have prototypes and fly around the base by Christmas."

His face grows crimson and his fork becomes a missile about to be fired. Twice, three times he bangs the tines against the plate and then points it at Dewhurst. "It's national security. It's freedom. It's the future. It's the whole American economy. I won't have the damn Russians, or some rich sheik or Ayatollah figure it out before we do. Let's pay a visit to our little friend Adam. Let's see if he'll listen to gentle persuasion."

Ever since the Adam headlines hit the internet Dewhurst has been expecting the General to have a meltdown and is surprised it has taken this long. Instead of troops to command, the General sits behind a desk at the Pentagon, flush with money to spend and nothing to show. Research project Titan is a blot on his career, with potential to premature retirement in disgrace, not getting him the position on the Joint Chiefs of Staff he craves. As long as he could keep saying it's impossible, no one has ever flown on his own, it cannot be done, he had a supportable position. But Adam has blown that one up. He's doing it. Every day on a TV screen or in a new viral video, Adam flies like an eagle, soars, swoops, glides over the Grand Canyon. The kid has guts and grace. But the General will have a coronary if he does not get the secret. And Dewhurst knows the meeting will not go well, has to get messy. Dewhurst wonders if this is his time to retire from the Army, take a job with a private contractor. He wouldn't miss Washington. He could get used to the sun of Arizona.

"It might be better, General, to deal with it softly, low-key, without scaring the kid and his entourage, without getting our interest splashed in the press. He's surrounded like Elvis and if we go in with a staff car and an armed force, it might make us look bad."

"Goddamn it, Dewhurst, don't patronize me. There is a time for negotiation, for nicey-nicey, for feints, but the best part of any war is the invasion. Shock and awe. This is war, Dewhurst. My troops are about to land on the beachhead and destroy the enemy. I am going to wipe out all resistance. I am in charge."

Dewhurst begins mentally going through old contacts and brushing up that résumé. "Yes, sir."

The sergeant at the wheel of the General's staff car is too experienced to squeal the tires, but his "Yes, Sir" to the General's command is crisp. "Won't meet with us," the General mutters under his breath. "Mom does not like the military," he wheedles, in imitation of an unbroken teenage voice. "This is the US goddam Army. You think we give a rat's ass what you or your mother like?"

Off the deep end, Dewhurst thinks. Totally unhinged. I wonder if I should notify the White House. Would the President's aide-de-camp talk to me? Not likely. The General is going kamikaze; it's D-Day. God help us.

Don't Wait Up

by Rachel Ambrose

I knew it would happen eventually. My first big fight with Blake erupted last night like pus out of a boil, forceful and messy and gross. As I wake up, flinging my hair out of my half open eyes, taking in the wreckage of my bedroom, mountains of dirty clothes on the floor, half-drunk cups of tea on the dresser, I can feel a migraine starting in the back of my head. Not a great way to start a morning full of family interaction, that's for sure.

And it's the first day of the annual family trip out to River Rock, where all fourteen of us rent a huge vacation mansion for a week. We inevitably eat, drink and smoke too much (overindulgence, when we don't have anywhere to be, is a Worthington family trait). I pull myself out of bed and glance at my phone. No calls or texts from Blake, but with the magnitude of the fight we had last night (I can still feel the tears behind my eyes, probably the cause of the migraine), I'd be a fool to expect any. He'll probably break up with me now, but honestly I've been preparing for that since day one. Then again, love without the fear of loss isn't really love, is it?

As I dress in my signature sweatpants and ancient t-shirt and pack the paltry amount of clean clothes I can find on my floor, I think to myself, stupid, stupid, stupid. The fight last night had stemmed from that horrible Jackie from last month's barn party – she got under my skin somehow, and then she always managed to be around, meeting us for brunch, trying to come over and watch movies, inviting herself out with us, just … underfoot. She made me feel itchy. And then last night I exploded all over Blake about it, and his feelings got hurt, because he really does like Jackie, they're friends and all, and he couldn't understand why I disliked her so – "honestly, you're ridiculous, we're just friends!" he said to me on more than one occasion. Maybe I am ridiculous, I consider as I zip my tote bag shut and write a note for Isa, who's moved back in, much to my delight (the epic snack buyer returns!). *Off to River Rock for the week,* the note says. *Don't wait up.*

My sister Molly picks me up in her fabulous silvery BMW. She's a lawyer, and she's done rather well for herself, and she's so progressive – did I mention she's also a lesbian? Girl power, indeed. I slide into the passenger seat after putting my tote in the back, roll my eyes up into my head, and announce, "If someone doesn't get me a vodka and an Extra Strength Tylenol as soon as we step foot in River Rock, I'm going to shit in everybody's hats."

Molly laughs as we turn off my street, brown eyes alight, blonde hair messy as always. "I'll pass that on to Mom and Dad. Tell 'em to hide their hats. Because either you must have a lot of shit inside you, or else you're counting on there being, like, precisely two hats."

As we drive along, I spill to her about the whole Blake fiasco, and she sits there tutting after I'm through. I pinch the bridge of my nose as a throb of pain explodes through my head. "What?" I demand when she stays quiet.

"Well, it's just …" she stops and starts. "I mean …" A sigh. "Blake does not seem like the kind of guy you need to be with. That's it! That's all I'm saying," she says, shooting me a defensive look. "He seems really high maintenance. All these fancy parties and hangers-on and 'ooh, I just love your work'. Why can't you just work on you for a change?"

she continues. "Take some Pilates, start drawing again like you used to do when you were younger. Join a book club, I don't know."

I blink at her, mouth a little agape. "A book club? Really, Molls? I know you're all about the virtues of the independent woman, but does every woman have to be independent? Why can't I just marry some rich artist and be able to eat bonbons and watch daytime TV all the time?"

"Why is that your greatest aspiration?" she shoots back. "To be able to do absolutely nothing of consequence with your life. Even if you did marry some rich douchebag, you could make your own art, have affairs, take classes, whatever. You could have some agency."

"It's not nothing," I reply quietly. My ears are ringing, although from anger or pain, I can't tell. "It's stability." My words are coming out slow and clipped. "It's about ... being able to breathe. It's about –" I take a deep breath to keep the shake from my voice, "finally having some guarantees. Because nothing scares me more than the unknown."

We ride in silence after that, and the familiar crunch of the BMW's tires on the gravel driveway at River Rock jolts me out of a sleep-like state I didn't even know I was in.

Too Late

by Gill Hoffs

Daughter mode is different when it's for real. No baby-talk, no perking my arse up for a slap if I've been 'naughty', no sitting on laps and wriggling on hard-ons. Just nodding in the right places, the mildest of swearing, and remembering to take a plate to catch the crumbs from her biscuits.

My aunt bakes for me when she knows I'm coming over. Anzac biscuits and solid scones and currant buns with flowery wrappers and bits that get stuck in my teeth. My mum would like to, but she knows Dad's sister would fret around us, tallying whose products I ate more of, interrupting us with questions of taste and comments about oven shelving as we attempt to sit in silence and blow on our cups of tea.

I wear sweaters or hoodies, no makeup, no heels. None of my work jewellery or undies, not after the time I squatted to rub Dumpling's freckled belly as she lay by the fire and my little brother twanged the crassly-bejewelled T of my G-string and drew it to Mum's attention. Cue a string of questions I didn't want to answer about whether there was a Special Someone in my life. Cue hints and sighs from my aunt about Not Leaving Love Too Late, Settling Down Before It Was Too Late, Not Being Too Picky in case it became Too Late, and the perils of spreading my fancies Too Freely. A little Too Late for that.

Dad sits on the mantelpiece as always, a vigorous dusting away from a tragedy and yet another bodged reclamation from the vacuum cleaner. I think Mum would be happier with the urn elsewhere, a garden of remembrance (I hate the implication that the dead would be forgotten otherwise) or thrown into the canal. Not like unwanted puppies in a suitcase or rubbers after a session under the bridge. He loved it there, fishing for perch, listening to the traffic rushing past, watching for bodies. But his sister leaks tears when we mention it, so he stays above the fireplace, rounded and dusty, when he was neither while living.

Conversation is limited, and whenever it looks like Mum or Auntie Michelle or Jay want to talk, I mean *properly* talk, I sniff and pull a tube of lozenges from my pocket (kept there for this very reason) and feign a cough while exuding menthol vapours. So far it's worked. I go home, everything stays polite and jokey and impersonal and manageable, I smile and nod and eat what they give me and pretend to relax, then get back in the car or onto the train and away again, phew!

Sometimes I think I'll just tell them.

Sometimes I think they already know.

But then someone yawns or sighs or turns the TV onto a talent show and Auntie Michelle mutters "Foolish little tarts" and no-one looks my way or pointedly doesn't, and I think maybe I'll tell Mum, maybe at bedtime, maybe when she brings a cup of tea and a sneaky shop-bought biscuit to my room in the morning, but then she smiles and it could be a decade ago when I've nowhere to escape to but the shops or school and the only thing that's been between my legs apart from tampons and 100% cotton gussets is the detachable showerhead and there's nothing I can tell her that would keep things the same.

I don't work as I do because Dad died. I wanted this job before that, before the cough and the cancer and the

46

hospital bed, before I even left school for Uni. I just hadn't known how or where or who to talk to so I could go about it. I scoured the local rag in vain for details of busts and madams fined in court, for small adverts placed before the massage parlours and chatlines and intimate services offered if you called a mobile number at so much per minute. I even sat, with my hair straightened by my mum's iron and my thighs shaved above my hold-ups, on benches near art gallery functions and celebratory lunches at museums and the town hall, in case I was mistaken for a 'date' and got my 'in' that way. A middle-aged woman who smelled of pear drops and piss offered me a boiled sweet and muttered something about "bastards" and being "stood up", so I went home.

Auntie Michelle is fluttering about in the kitchen, opening the oven door instead of peering through the glass, letting the heat out so the kitchen smells great but the chicken will take longer than necessary. Jay rolls his eyes at me and I wink and sit cross-legged beside Dumpling on the rug, rubbing her belly in circles till my eyes sting with fart. She raises her head, glances back at the guilty area, wags her tail – no! don't wave it at me! – and licks my knee.

Jay flicks my ear with his fingers as he walks past on his way to his room to 'study'. I suspect he's just pissing about online, but it's his life and I don't really give a fuck.

With Jay gone, it's just me and Mum and Dumpling in the living room. There's another couple of hours till the usual round of soaps start on the box, summer has forgotten to unleash its heat on the north of England, and rain is tapping on the windows as if it wants to come in.

Mum leans forward on the settee, elbows on knees, and smiles at me with her lips tucked in.

"I need to talk to you about something."

"Oh?"

Dumpling snuggles against me and I feign calm, easing rumples of fat from around her collar, poking them underneath with my finger instead of leaping up to extricate the lozenges from my pocket.

"You know I've been unwell."

I shake my head, and gulp, and realise this isn't about the escort work.

"I've been to the doctors a few times, and the hospital – just for tests, things like that. And it's nothing too awful, nothing hereditary or anything like that."

"Well, what is it?"

I'm staring at her and realise her eyes are yellow where there should only be white, and she's lost weight, and my vision closes in so there is only her to see. My hand keeps stroking Dumpling but the rest of me is still.

"I have to have an operation, a small one. It's nothing too dreadful, they won't fillet me, it's all keyhole. But it's got me thinking and I want to pass some things to you now, just to set my mind at rest."

"When?"

"Now, I have them right here, ready for you comi–"

I shake my head.

"No. Mum, the operation. When's your operation?"

"Next week. Wednesday. All being well, as it will be, I'll be home for the weekend."

I blink. It must be serious if they're doing it so soon.

"Do you want me to take you in? Talk to the nurses and doctors, make sure you get the nice ones?"

I can feel my nose producing misery-mucus, wet and trickling inside, and sniff before something dribbles out and reveals my upset when I'm trying my damnedest to be adult about my only parent getting sick.

She leans over and hooks my hair behind my ears with her index finger. No hiding now.

"I wasn't telling you to worry you, and I don't need any help. Your Auntie Michelle will keep Jay in tea and biscuits while I'm in hospital, and they've said it won't take long for me to feel like my old self again. But."

I don't like the pause, or how she stares into my eyes – I suspect she's steadying herself, and it makes my heart race and throb in my throat.

"But?"

"But I like to be careful, so before I forget" – as if she would – "I want you to take these. I've been holding on to them for you anyway. They were your dad's and mine, when we were courting. Maybe you can give one to your own special someone."

And she holds out two narrow silver bands.

I slip one on each index finger, working by feel alone as I daren't look down in case gravity betrays the tears balancing on my lower lash-line, and she sits back in her chair, smiling with her lips visible, clearly more at ease.

I sniff again, and open my mouth to say something but then Auntie Michelle drops something with a clatter and a smash and squeals out a 'No!' and Mum rolls her eyes and rushes out to help.

And the moment to connect with her has gone.

From the comments in the kitchen, and Mum calling through to me, "You like mustard with your chicken sometimes, don't you?" I gather the gravy jug's gone, too.

Tuesday, stringbeans

by Susan Tepper

The shower water is too fricking hot – scalds his backside. Why do they have to call it ass or butt? he's thinking. Heine! Now there was a good one! Clean your heine, the grownups used to say. Pedersen spits the toothpaste at his feet.

He likes the all-in-one shower. The army called it 3 S's: shit, shower and shave. You got three minutes. There were times he had to creep into the latrine at night and dig the shit out of his ass. That gave him a little extra time for the shower and shave. The army. Someone should bomb the shit out of the army. Pedersen gargles shower water watching the rivulets swirl around the drain.

Summer is about to spring. The kiddies will be packed off to camps across America. Schoolyards will be dead except for teenagers who got left back for being dumber than shit. His little darlings will be gone until the fall. Those sweet things – their soft rosy cheeks and bony scraped knees.

He sees Swoon the white rat and picks it up by the tail swinging it. The rat squeals, little high-pitched sounds, little legs scurrying in the air. "You s'posed to stay in your hole till I play the special music," he tells it.

Dropping the rat, Pedersen wipes steam off the bathroom mirror. He rubs his stubble looking closely at himself in the glass. *Not a fine specimen* crosses his mind.

"Vegetables," he says, remembering that jingle from childhood: Monday *something*, Tuesday stringbeans, Wednesday soooooouuuppp. Do I really love ya? Ya bet I do.

He'll boil a pot of stringbeans. Good for the virility. It is important to maintain virility at all costs.

You lose your balls in combat, you're a dead man, the sergeant told Pedersen during basic training. He remembered it. It wasn't the sort of thing you'd soon forget. This association: death and his balls.

His little darlings have balls the size of Swoon, practically. Tiny little balls meant for cupping and holding. They run around the schoolyard with their little balls, little pricks. He could help them learn to piss correctly. He could help them become men.

The white rat runs across the tub edge. "Get the frick out of here you scummy white prick you leavin' rat shit on my clean tub."

Pedersen takes a tissue and brushes the rat droppings into the tub, running the shower to wash them away.

"It can be that easy," he says.

Wednesday, 11th June 2014

First Class

by Jessica McHugh

Edward is meant to be a lion today – proud, authoritative, strong but graceful. But as he stands before thirteen eighth graders longing to enjoy their summer instead of being cooped up in a classroom, Father Edward McKenzie is a wounded zebra at their carnivorous mercy.

He clears his throat, adjusts his crucifix on his chest, and exhales, glad they can't see his skin prickling beneath his vestments – or the rosy camisole he'd donned that morning to boost his confidence. He wasn't sure he'd need it, but standing in front of the class, his hands shaking, he's glad for the feeling of secret satin.

"Welcome to your first summer session of Health Studies," he announces. "We'll be meeting every Wednesday and Friday at 10am sharp for the next four weeks, discussing all sorts of health topics, from mental and physical to sexual."

Several kids yawn. Some tap their pens on their desks and scribble in their notebooks.

Writing his name on the chalkboard, he continues. "I see some familiar faces, but for those of you I don't know, my name is Father McKenzie." He faces the classroom. "I've been a priest at St. Peter's for about thirty years now, and I'm eager to get to know all of you."

A boy raises a waving hand, his words spilling out after Edward's acknowledging nod.

"I've heard about you," he says, his tone pointed. "You're the one with the drunk mom who killed someone … your grandmother?"

"That …" His voice squeaks, and he lowers his head. His throat is parched, and his camisole is wet under his armpits.

You're in charge here, Edward. Don't let fear rule your life.

Looking up, he sees Grandma Eleanor at the back of the classroom, dressed in flowing pink chiffon, gliding between the desks. The aroma of her Duska powder thickens, as she places her hand on his shoulder.

I'm here for you. For as long as you need me.

Edward nods and clears his throat. "That was a long time ago," he tells the boy. "And it's not pertinent to Health Studies."

"I don't know what pertinent means, but I'd think someone who was raised by a drunken murderer doesn't know much about being healthy." The kid laughs as he turns to his classmate. "Am I right?"

Edward faces the chalkboard as air fires from his lungs. He's dizzy, and his chest aches. He longs to lean his head against the board and pretend thirteen kids aren't staring at him. The boy has stopped talking, but a voice persists in Edward's mind, spat from the cracked lips of Betty McKenzie.

"What do you know about health, Edward?" his mother asks. "What kind of teacher, what kind of priest, what kind of *man* wears a satin cami under his clothes?" He exhales a shuddering breath, his fists clenched. His mother stands behind him, her boozy words hot on the back of his neck. "You're no man," she says. "And you're sure as hell no teacher. You're an abomination."

"You're wrong," Edward says. He spins around, catching the students' shocked expressions. "What you know about me isn't really about me, but about people who sought to poison my life. But I won't let that happen anymore. Not from my mother, and certainly not from you, son. Do you understand?"

The boy gawks, his brow furrowed. When the student sitting behind him leans forward to tap his shoulder, Father Edward recognizes the boy as Nelson Wade, one of the altar boys at St. Peter's. The unruly kid looks back at the glare Nelson fires, and facing front again, lowers his gaze and nods slowly.

"Good. I'm glad we got that cleared up," Edward says. "Now, everyone, please open your Health Studies books to chapter one: 'Overcoming Inner Obstacles'."

Grandma Eleanor stands at the back of the classroom and smiles, but by the time every textbook smacks open on their desks, she's gone. The only powder Edward inhales is the Duska on his own skin.

A Mark on the Armour

by Shane Simmons

Slumping down on the sofa, I notice the clear plastic crate which Aunt Patricia and Uncle John had brought over on Sunday. It was one of the last few I'd neglected to take with me when I'd moved out. Hauling it up, I place it on the sofa beside me.

I prise the lid open and get a whiff of stale air, the smell of papers left in storage. And there are stacks of papers. I don't recognise them immediately and so shuffle my fingers between the sheets to find they're nothing particularly important, old college work, the odd photo, test prints, contact sheets. I pull out an unmarked brown envelope from the back and peer inside.

Pouring out a pile of 6" x 4" prints onto my lap, I flick through them. Each still life conjures half-memories of walking around for hours, weekends avoiding the silent tension and inevitable blow-ups at home, all the while seeking that elusive shot.

At the back of the set I stop. It stares back at me.

It was taken just up the road from the family home. In the background, rays from the London summer sun streaming through leafy branches.

Just what I meant to capture is beyond my recollection. But the instant he jumped out in front of the camera plays in my mind so clearly.

I shiver as a chill travels down my spine and the photo trembles in my hands.

Here he is, imperfections in stark sharpness.

I jump out of my skin as there's a rap on the window. I'd forgotten Sandra was coming over to borrow my old DVD player. I toss the photos into the box, throw on the lid and pop it down on the floor beside the sofa.

"Your buzzer still not working?" she asks as she steps across the threshold. "And what's the matter with you? You look like you've seen a ghost!"

"You startled me."

She stops just inside the living room door, "Can't stay long, Marlon will be wanting his dinner!"

I pick up the bag from in front of the TV and hand it over to her: it rustles in my hands.

"I didn't give you that much of a fright did I? You're trembling! Not had enough wine tonight?" she smirks.

I walk over to the window, and pull the curtains shut.

"You're acting stranger than usual … s'pose I *could* stay for a bit." As she plonks herself down on the sofa she spots the crate on the floor. And points. "What's in there?"

"Just old college stuff."

"*So* …" her voice chimes up and down, "who's that?" She reaches down and lifts off the lid.

I leap over to stop her, but she already has the photos in her hand.

"Hmm, not a bad looking guy!" She turns to stare me up and down. "College *friend*?"

"Leave it be, Sandra."

"Come on, you can tell aunty Sand!"

I burst like a water balloon hitting the pavement. Through a film of saltwater that clouds my eyes I see Sandra freeze, eyes wide … then she sprints out of the room and returns with a half-used toilet roll and unwinds some before handing it over to me.

Much nose blowing and messy snivelling later she whispers, "Want to talk about it?"

I shake my head.

"Are you sure? Because Marlon can wait for his dinner." She waves the photo in front of me. "Is this what's upset you?"

I nod.

"So, what's his name?"

It's been years since his name passed my lips. "Mark."

"Mark? Well that's very 'normal'. God, even I went out with a Mark once. So, what's so upsetting about this Mark? Did he … he didn't pass away, did he?"

"He may as well have."

"Oh. It's like that."

She heads to the sofa and puffs the limp cushions before beckoning me over. I sit down and wipe my face down with my palms.

"They are all bastards, aren't they?" She pats me on the back like a well-behaved dog.

"End of our first college year, he just disappeared, fucked off. No goodbye, no explanation, all that time he'd just strung me along." I stop. And sniff. "I really thought he fucking cared about me!"

"Fucking bastards, all of them!"

I nod in agreement and feel like I've been initiated into that exclusive 'All men are bastards' club, the one that only the bitterest and most scorned get to join.

"Have you ever told anyone about this 'Mark' before?"

I shake my head.

"And you've never been with anyone since? Sheesh. Well, I reckon it's high time you moved on. We're going to find you someone! You can't go through the rest of your life celibate as a monk, all because of this Mark twat."

She picks up the photo and begins to tear it in two.

"NO!" I yell.

She stops, and places it down on the coffee, the photo ripped a centimetre in from the edge.

"You're going to have to let go someday, you can't hold onto memories forever. It's not healthy."

Her phone blares a brash tone from her pocket.

"Marlon's wondering where I am. Look, I better get going, but I have a plan …"

"What plan?"

"I was just thinking. There's a work do next month, to celebrate the end of the A&E refurb. Big party, loads of people going. We're gonna go out shopping, I'll choose you some new, *stylish* clothes, and you're going to come to this do with me and I'm going to introduce you to all the gays! One of them will like you, surely!"

"Oh god no –"

"Don't … you … dare!" She jabs my arm with each word. "You're going, that's that." She pats my arm, "You know it's time."

I can't argue with her when she's actually coming across with genuine concern. Who'd have thought it?

I raise my eyebrows and nod.

"That's settled. Because I know I said they're all bastards but at least they're good for *one* thing. And no one should be without *that* for as long as you have!"

She picks up the DVD player and heads out to the hall. "You'll be alright, I'll make sure of that. God, I wish you'd told me all this months ago, I could've had you set up with a nice new lay by now!"

Walking back into the living room after letting her out, the first thing I see is that photo, staring at me. The grin that lured me in. I should tear it up. Set it on fire.

I pick it up, slide it back into the envelope it came from and stuff the envelope down the back of the crate.

I might want to take it out, look at it again.

Trace my finger over the contours of his face. Look into those hazel eyes, one more time.

Friday, 13th June 2014

Daffodils

by Michelle Elvy

"I'm leaving," says Stevie, and when he says it, it sounds as if he's been waiting to say this for a long, long time.

"I know." Manny's been Stevie's best friend since they were kids, and he's known this moment would come from the day they met. Stevie never seemed like he really *belonged* here. He was always a little outside the rest of them. On the soccer field he played left forward, and as Manny watched from the sidelines while Stevie charged lightning fast after the ball he sometimes thought Stevie might just keep on running, over the line and off the field, never looking back. Even later, when they outgrew junior soccer and started jacking cars and driving too fast and smoking too much weed – even then, Stevie was there but *not* there. But Manny had never begrudged him this. There was something out there pulling Stevie away, ever since Manny could remember.

Manny would have found it beyond strange if Stevie stayed.

"Where you goin'?" They are lying on the old pier down by the river, their graduation gowns crumpled in a pile. It's a blistering June day, and they are stripped down to their boxers now, lying side-by-side, arms and legs spread-eagle, as they've done so many days during so many summers.

"Dunno. Florida, maybe."

"The Sunshine State."

"Yeah."

"What about college? Aren't your parents expecting you to go get some *higher education*?" Manny says it with great emphasis. *Higher Education*. Like he doesn't quite believe there's more to learn after the torture of high school Algebra and French. Not for him anyway. The only way he expects to set foot on a university campus is to visit his friend for some seriously good parties and maybe a night or two with a college girl. And Vermont seems like a cool place for a roadtrip.

"I deferred. Middlebury said it's OK. And my parents think it's a good idea."

"Your parents have no idea what kind of trouble you'll get into in Florida, do they?"

Stevie grinned. "Not as much trouble as I would if you were along."

"True. But you didn't invite me, did you?"

"Look ..."

"Hey, I'm just bustin' you. It's cool. You go on. I'll point my wheels south when it's time for a road trip. Girls wear less clothes in Florida, right? I'll come in the winter when my tits are froze."

The boys lie in the sun without speaking while a fly buzzes lazily by Manny's face and a butterfly lands on the corner of a graduation cap. Water laps gently at the pilings below. Manny lights up and passes the joint.

"Whatever happened between Ellie and Rick?" he says as he exhales. "You know ... after the crash."

"What do you mean?"

"Well you know, man, that blowjob – that was one to remember."

Stevie's mind roils and he's suddenly not here on the dock with his friend but in a cornfield in January, hurtling back through time. He arrives at the image he can't shake.

Again. Not the flash and mangled metal of a car flipped three times, not his friends banged and bruised. As much as the car crash has changed his life – as much as Lucky being dead has changed *everything* – the things that occurred moments before were just as indelible. And when Manny mentions the blowjob, a backward sequence is set in motion, one Stevie can't control: it begins with him lying in a cornfield, and then his face and back leave the crunchy frozen ground and he flies upward, from the cornfield toward the car. He passes his Uncle Gus on a tall ship in an inexplicable dreamscape he can't chase out of the sequence and floats there in a nanosecond of calm – no noise, no screams, no metal, no horn, no radio, no voices. Nothing. Then he's flying through the window into the back seat; he feels the impact and briefly, only for a moment then the moment's gone, he sees his friend Lucky turn his head and smile at him from the front seat. Now he looks over and sees Rick and Ellie, and he feels his stomach lurch. This is the thing he does not want to see. This is what doesn't make sense to him: Lucky's alive and smiling when he shouldn't be, and everything's out of joint. He sees that now. It's all fucked up. It's like the car crash is the last thing they all did together, but even in the moments before it, they weren't *really* together. And he's thought all this time that he was the only one to know about Ellie and Rick, but now Manny has said the unsayable. Manny has put a name on this thing he witnessed, and he feels sick all over again.

Manny takes another toke. "Seriously, did they ever hook up again? Even after Lucky … ?"

Stevie knows the answer to the question. Of course they didn't hook up. Ellie has been a wreck. He's pretty sure she never wants to see Rick again, and he longs for the day he hears her say it. Because he wants someone else to hate Rick as much as he does. And because he wants it to be true. It's all much more complicated than Manny thinks.

Because even Manny – his best friend – has no idea that Stevie is in love with Ellie.

"I mean, you know how fucked up I've been since the accident," Manny is pouring out his heart now, talking about the accident like he's never done before. Something about graduation day seems to have opened a floodgate. "I haven't been able to talk to Ellie, you know ..."

"She doesn't blame you."

"Well ..."

"I don't either."

"Yeah well, Lucky's folks do."

"They've got to blame someone, but it doesn't mean they mean it." Even as he says it, Stevie knows Lucky's parents will never get over blaming Manny. The boy who'd eaten PBJs at their kitchen table when he was twelve. The boy who'd built tents out of sheets in their backyard and flashed Morse code past midnight. The boy who'd cut their lawn. The boy who drove the car that broke their son's neck and bashed his brain in.

Manny's silence beside him is breaking Stevie's heart, so he says, "Listen, I'm proud of you for graduating."

"Thanks, Gramps."

"I mean it."

The silence between them stretches out until Manny recovers his bravado.

"Didn't think I would, did ya?"

"Wasn't too sure there for a while."

"That makes two of us, man."

The truth was, after the accident, most people thought Manny had dropped out of school entirely, even if some teachers had confided in Stevie about Manny, trying to keep him on track. There had been a couple months when Manny was MIA and even Stevie was not sure where he'd gone. The day of the funeral, after Lucky had lain in a coma nearly a month, was the one time Manny returned during February. Stevie had looked everywhere but never did figure out where he went. Then Manny showed up again in late April, and now he's here, cap and gown crumpled on the dock.

"I thought Justin's speech was pretty cool," Stevie adds now, thinking back to the graduation ceremony.

"Shit, man, you're not gonna say that out loud to anyone else, are you?"

"I'm just sayin' ... those speeches are usually a big fuckin' eye-roll, you know? But he said some pretty cogent things."

"Cogent, yes, Sherlock. Cogent."

Stevie laughs at Manny's grown-up voice. "Well you gotta admit, the part about the amphibious Martian was pretty funny."

"Yeah, he's not such a 'tard as I thought. Who woulda thought Justin Fuckin' Tucker could be funny and philosophical?"

Stevie's quiet for a moment. "I liked what he said about the daffodils on Lucky's grave, too."

He feels Manny tense next to him, then slowly exhale. He watches the branches sway back and forth overhead as the butterfly returns to the graduation cap and balances delicately on one corner. He pictures Lucky's grave with hundreds of daffodils over it. He's not been to the cemetery in ages, and he wonders if everyone else in the audience was as surprised as he was by what Justin had said – that one day a few weeks back daffodils sprang up all over the grave. Late in the season for daffodils. Strange. And amazing. He liked how Justin had talked about the strangeness of circumstances, the way unknowns can bring wonder, how beauty can be seen in the unlikeliest places. What Justin said about Lucky's life and Lucky's death was just this side of a Hallmark card. It was quite beautiful, really.

"Do you think it's true, or was he just making shit up?"

"Let's find out." Stevie knows Manny hasn't visited Lucky's grave, ever. Today – graduation day and Friday the 13th – feels like the right day.

"What – now?" Manny turns his head to face Stevie. He looks scared.

"Yeah." Stevie's voice is firm, unwavering. "Now."

"After a swim?"

"Alright."

"Lucky'd want us to jump in our graduation gowns."

"Lucky'd be proud of you today, too, you know."

"Lucky'd have called me chickenshit for not going full commando under the gown."

In a flash Stevie is on his feet and stripping off his boxers. He doesn't look back but he knows Manny is doing the same. In two giant steps he walks forward and propels himself off the end of the dock. The shallow water is warm and familiar. He comes up for air and turns just in time to see Manny jumping in naked, graduation cap balanced on his head. He sees the golden tassel fly up in the air as Manny splashes down. Then, only the cap can be seen on the surface of the water. Stevie watches it and marvels at his friend in this brief moment of profound silence, at all he's been through since the accident. The cap starts to fill with water. Stevie treads water but doesn't reach out to grab it. He wonders whether it will sink or remain just below the surface, but he decides it doesn't matter. Manny comes up with a giant gulp of air just as the cap capsizes.

Tomorrow Stevie will think about Florida, and about Ellie. He'll think about leaving Manny. He'll think about saying goodbye to his parents and his brother. He'll think about signing and posting the formal deferral letter to Middlebury College. He'll think about Ellie some more. He may even call her.

But today the only place he can be is here with Manny, floating, and then later, in the heat of the June evening, sitting cross-legged with Coronas in a field of yellow flowers that sprawl across a grave on the northeast corner of a Maryland cemetery.

Algorithms

by Len Kuntz

The gun dealer is a grizzled old man who brings along his Down's Syndrome son. We meet in a warehouse district somewhere on the outskirts of Albuquerque. The building is large and crowded and noisy with workers changing license plates and using sanders to scrape off registration numbers from various cars that have most likely been stolen.

"Isn't there some place private we can go?" I shout above the din.

The old guy shouts back, "Too risky."

His son wears a striped t-shirt with Neapolitan ice cream colors. His palms are pressed against his ears and he's grimacing as if constipated.

"Come on," I shout, "look at the poor kid."

The old man thinks it over, then leads us to a restroom in back. Every *Playboy* centerfold Pamela Anderson's ever been in is tacked to the walls, in addition to a spread from *Playgirl* featuring Burt Reynolds.

The old guy sets a trunk on a sink counter where, by the looks of the mess, someone's just recently had a bloody nose or worse. Not only are there red smears everywhere, but the faucet knobs are lined with grime and a broken toothbrush is stuck in the drain.

The old guy opens the trunk with a flourish, as if he's some kind of magician. Inside are a Rubik's Cube and two old pistols that look right out of the Civil War. He hands the cube to the kid and the kid tosses it in the air and misses catching it, picks it up from the floor and tosses it again, over and over.

"Not much of a selection," I say.

"What did you expect, machine guns? I ain't Walmart."

I buy the smaller pistol and a box of shells the old guy has in his coat pocket. Why he's wearing a jacket when it's an eighty-five degree June day is anybody's guess.

"Say, do you mind keeping an eye on Keith for a few minutes?"

Keith tosses the Rubik's cube and this time it lands in the toilet, water splashing over the rim, and he starts to bawl.

"Are you kidding?" I say.

"Just be a little while. Here, you can have the second gun free."

"Why do I need two?"

"You never know."

The old guy hands me the gun and heads out the door. I shout after him, but he doesn't stop. Keith is crying harder than ever. I reach into the toilet with its lemon-colored water and foist out the toy, washing it in the sink with globs of soap, then wiping my hands with my shirt tail.

A half an hour passes. An hour. The Rubik's Cube has a number of squares broken off and they lay like bright-colored Skittles on the filthy floor.

I start to panic. "Hey, Keith," I say, "where did Dad go? Or Granddad?"

Keith says something that sounds like hotdogs.

"He went to lunch, is that where Grandpa went?"

Then he says something that sounds like chili.

"Fuck me," I say, taking Keith's hand and heading out of the restroom, out of the shop and down the street where I'd seen a food truck earlier.

The guy manning the truck is the palest person I've ever seen, with a dandelion seed afro that could match anything Art Garfunkel ever sported. "What'll you have?"

I ask him if he's seen the old guy, but Art says he hasn't. When I ask him if he knows Keith, he looks at me like I'm nuts.

"This isn't my kid," I say. "He belongs to the old guy."

"And that's my problem, why?"

"Look, I really need to get going. Do you mind watching the boy Keith? His grandfather dropped him off with me at that shop across the block and he'll be right back."

"Are you on meth?"

"I'll give you a gun," I say, pulling the pistol out of my pocket.

"Whoa!"

"No, I'm giving it to you, free."

When I try handing the pistol across the counter the guy dips and comes back up holding a shotgun.

"Drop it."

"Hey, it's not like that."

"I'll plaster your face with pellets if you don't drop your weapon."

"That's just it, I was trying to give it to you as payment for watching Keith."

Keith reaches up and snatches the pistol. I see my opportunity and sprint behind the food truck and keep running until I'm in my car.

As I drive, the remaining pistol chafes my inner thigh, and when I pull it out two chips from the Rubik's Cube clatter against the stick shift.

I feel shitty for abandoning Keith but I tell myself he's better off with a food truck guy than me. I replay the events of the day in my head trying to figure out where I went wrong but after a while the road opens up to a land so flat that it's hypnotic the way watching a campfire is, and my thoughts dull as I roll down the window to let the air in, warm wind whipping my hair like a set of groping fingers.

Sixth Inning

by Michael Webb

It happens so quickly that I register it more than actually seeing it. I kick and throw, and the hitter for Los Angeles, Alex Sellers, is not fooled for an instant, turning on the ball, which I threw too high and horribly flat, drilling it. Fortunately for my continued reproductive potential, he started his swing a fraction too soon, not hitting it back at my body but instead to my right, near the third base bag but, luckily, foul. Our third baseman, a former college basketball player we call 'Hammer', dives for the ball anyway, his effort spoiled when the umpire barks, "Foul!"

I let my breath out in a rush. The Baseball Gods don't let you get away with those too often. He should have hit that ball to Space Mountain. I wait for Graham, our massive third sacker, to haul his long body off the ground, and then, when he catches my eye, I flick my gloved hand at him, semaphore for "Appreciate the effort, Big Man." Graham nods, flipping the ball back to me before nonchalantly dusting his uniform off and getting himself back together. I give him a moment to recover, another unwritten rule, ball tucked securely away, removing my hat and slicking back my sweaty hair.

Everyone pauses for a moment, a frozen tableau of inaction. The plate umpire stands back, squinting in the hot sun. My catcher, Hector Cruz, straightens up, looks at me through the bars of his mask as he makes the devil horns symbol, reminding us all that there are two outs. I mentally review the situation as I take the ball into my throwing hand. Two on, two out, Two and two count, what my youth baseball coach called 'The Woolery', a joke I wouldn't get for years. I stare at the ump, waiting for him to ask for the ball and check it for imperfections. Distracted, he makes no sign, so I climb the hill and prepare to go back to work.

Hector kneels again and flashes his symbols. We are thinking along the same lines, going away next, then, if that fails, trying to finish him inside. If that doesn't work, as our manager joked during the pre-game discussion about how to handle the red hot Los Angeles team, we will try prayer. My fingertips find the tiny imperfection in the ball's cover as I rub it up. My heart leaps as I feel the ridge. Every schoolboy who has thrown a tattered ball knows that an interruption in the ball's smooth surface affects the flow of air, thus causing lift and a ball that darts like a Whiffle Ball. Totally illegal, but used since the beginning of time just the same. Anything, in the evolutionary struggle of offense and defense, to get an advantage, no matter how small. Honest? No. But in a profession where fractions of inches mean millions of dollars, every advantage, to a man, to a father, must be taken and held. They'd do the same to me, if they could.

I get up onto the rubber, and the whole mechanism starts again. Signals, offensive and defensive. Look at the runners. Pause, look, then tilt and kick and throw. The trick comes through for me, Bernoulli's principle, the same rule that provides lift to an airplane, yields a slider that starts almost behind Sellers, breaking like a Frisbee to the opposite side of the plate, a pitch so nasty he can only wave meekly at it, Cruz catching the ball and pumping his fist once on the way to the dugout, the LA fans groaning at the rally snuffed out.

"What the fuck was that?" Cruz says into my ear as we come down the steps. "That was some good shit."

He opens his glove and goes to throw the ball back on the field. I put my hand on his wrist, then wordlessly turn the ball over, showing him the cut in the ball's surface.

"I didn't know you did that," Cruz says softly.

"I don't," I say. "It happened naturally. On the foul ball the pitch before."

"But you threw it."

"Yeah," I say. I have a spasm of shame, remembering my moralizing about Tex and whatever that was he injected into himself that gray day in Kansas City.

"Oh," he says, tossing the ball down the dark hall that leads to the clubhouse, towards an open bag. "Whatever it takes, right?"

I mentally tabulate the runs saved, estimate the cost to my salary next year if I throw a legal ball instead and Sellers bounces it off the Hollywood sign. "Whatever it takes," I agree.

Man's Best Friend

by James Claffey

Another June Monday full of rain showers and leaking roofs, the Bird thinks, as he sets the pail in the centre of the bedroom floor and captures the ringing drips from the cracked plaster above. Since May he's spent most days stuck in the house, afraid to venture outside for fear of ridicule. God, how he hated the gobshites who had poked fun at him in McKettrick's bar, and the barking that now follows him around the town whenever he slips out to get the messages, or to go to Mass on a Sunday.

The dusty statues and paintings left by his parents are only irritations to him as he tries to protect the carpet from the steady drips of rain. The statues and paintings could be watching him in his shameful misery as he stumbles from one day of his difficult life to the next. He knows, though, that the priest is right about the townsfolk's ridicule. He told him to pay them no mind, and that they were no better than the Pharisees in the temple, and they'd little right to judge a man without understanding the circumstances, or jumping to conclusions the way they had.

"I'll go down to McKettrick's tonight, by God. They won't get the better of the Bird," he says, as he places a saucepan under another leak.

The kitchen depresses the Bird, his mother's pots and pans, the old Player's cigarettes ashtray with the pipe-smoking sailor, the rusted biscuit tin where she used to keep the flour, and the statue of the Madonna of Prague with its billowing skirts. A bloody jumble sale, that's what he should have and clear her memory out of the house good and proper. He tried to do it the month following her death, but his father had taken sick by that time and the Bird didn't have the heart or the time to arrange everything. Now, though, that the two of them are gone, he's better placed to get a good start on the job, but only after his afternoon constitutional by the river and a pint or two in McKettrick's snug later.

Funny how the shadows manage to appear at all times of day and night, too. Wasn't he only after settling down with the wireless on Radio Four's 'Book at Bedtime' and his father's stooped back and jug ears had appeared on the sitting room wall? When he'd blinked again the shadow had passed and the hum of the wireless was the only sound in the house. A lonely man he is now, in his big old house next door to the convent, and the French girl away out of it, and bound never to speak to him again once she hears about the curious incident with the dog in the telephone box.

Forever ago, all the laughter and tears of his parents' marriage had filled the house like great ricks of hay in the nearby fields. Only *their* shadows. Only the odd letter or card from a distant friend who'd not heard of their deaths ever hit the carpet, now. "A terrible thing to be growing old," his father often told him. Now, with the wrinkles on his own face resembling a contour map of the local mountains, he knows exactly what his father was talking about.

On the way out the door he dips two of his fingers in the waterless Holy Water fount and dryly blesses himself. Outside, the west wind whips leaves in circles on the road and crows battle against the breeze as they make their way home for the evening. He pushes the Raleigh along, and when the moment is right, swings aboard and heads for the towpath by the canal. Not many are out and about today, and he says a silent blessing for their scarcity. All he needs is a few blackguards yelping and barking at him.

To the lamppost he locks the bicycle and hangs both trouser clips off the handlebars. Not much in the way of fish biting in the water, he sees. Mayflies catch what's left of the sun's rays, and across on the other bank a terrier scrabbles frantic at a hole in the undergrowth. The Bird envies the dog its energy and makes his way along the towpath. This is a walk his father took of an evening, after dinner and before the Mart & Market report on the wireless. The Bird allows his father's spirit to descend on him, almost like a mantle, and he struggles to recall anything at all of the subjects that mattered to his father. Most of their time spent together was in a companionable silence, the weighty conversations took place in his imagination, wishing the words into his father's mouth.

As he walks along the muddied path he marvels at how the pattern of holes cut into the leather of his brogues is so symmetrical, and remembers the day his father took him on the train to Belfast to collect the shoes from Cable & Company's offices. The first time he tried on the shoes after his father's death he noticed how his feet perfectly matched the grooves worn by his father's feet over those forty years since their trip to Belfast. In a whisper, searching the vicinity for nearby walkers, he mimics his father's voice, saying, "A man's best friend is a pair of decent shoes." The surge of sadness almost knocks the Bird off his feet, and he has to steady himself by sitting on a stone bench surrounded by dandelions and broken beer bottles.

Across the sky vapor trails of planes bound for America fade in front of his eyes. A holiday, perhaps. He's always wanted to visit New York and the Statue of Liberty, and to walk in Central Park. So far, the farthest away he's managed to make it is a weekend in Galway with the Pioneer Society when he was only a teenager and a devout teetotaler. He'd learned a quick lesson that trip, what with the secret drinking of the leaders of the society; men who wore their Pioneer pins proudly and never stopped boasting of their devotion to not drinking, and the long gash he'd gotten on the sole of his foot the time he jumped off the pier and landed on a jagged beer bottle.

"Bird," a voice calls out, and fast approaching from the near dark is Father O'Hehir, a blackthorn stick in one hand and his breviary in the other.

"Father, a grand summer's day, isn't it?"

"How are you lately?" the priest stops and stares at the Bird, his thick-browed eyes dark as the river water.

"Game ball. I'm clearing out some belongings from the house. Things the parents left behind."

"A fine plan. Out with the old and in with the new."

A minute of silence and the priest coughs twice and says, "Did I hear you'd gotten yourself an Alsatian dog, or something of that sort?"

The Bird reddens under the collar and curses the tattletales in McKettrick's. "No, Father. It was all a bit of a mistake."

"Now, Bird, grief is a terrible thing to deal with alone. You can always come down to the church if you're having trouble of a personal nature, if you know what I mean." The priest lays the hand with the breviary on the Bird's shoulder and a shock travels down the Bird's body as if he's been electrocuted.

"Not at all, Father. I'm doing grand as things stand," the Bird says, brushing past the priest and on towards the far end of the towpath. He wishes his bike were waiting for him so he could pedal the hell off to the bar and not even think about the disastrous rumors he is sure will follow him to his grave. Small bloody towns and interfering bloody priests. "And I'll be damned if I come to the church for any reason at all," he almost shouts after the priest, but is careful to let the words fall silent into the dark canal water.

It's About Time Somebody Died

by Gwendolyn Joyce Mintz

"So, what are we celebrating?" Lindsey, their server, asks as she sets the flutes of champagne before those seated at the table.

"One of our members has reached the club goal," Aaron says.

Her eyes scan the group. "Which of you?"

"In absentia," Aaron adds.

"Oh, well, still, congrats," Lindsey says, lifting an imaginary glass in the air.

When she walks away, Mora, sitting at Aaron's left, turns to him and asks, "What're you talking about? We're all here."

By the glass stem, Aaron spins the flute in a slow circle. "Vincent killed himself," he says.

It is Mora who breaks the silence that follows Aaron's words. "How do you know?"

"I kept in touch with him. He liked the idea of the club." He glances at Mora, then across the table to Phil and Diane. "I think of him as an honorary member." He lifts his glass. "To Vincent Lawrence DiMatteo."

The others hesitate then with uncertainty, they too raise their glasses, clink, drink.

"It's about time somebody died," Phil says, setting the flute down. "I was beginning to think that was never gonna happen."

"How'd he do it?" Diane asks, then immediately says, "No, no, never mind. I don't want to know."

"He wanted you to know that he was sorry you were offended by what he said."

Diane raises a brow. "But not sorry for what he said." She shakes her head, then tosses it back, downing the champagne. She sets the flute down with a thunk. "I'm glad he's dead."

Aaron's smile is wry. "So am I." He leans back against the booth seating. "He was an introvert, Diane. Very much so. He was hoping that joining this desperate bunch craving death, well, not you so much," he says as an aside to Mora, "would allow him a chance to relate to people. He didn't mean any harm."

"Did you go to his funeral?"

Aaron doesn't turn to look at Mora. He stares at a spot in the center of the table.

"You did!" Mora exclaims. "I thought –"

She stops because Lindsey returns with a tray of wings, celery sticks, and Ranch dressing.

"We didn't order this," Aaron says as she begins passing out small plates and napkins.

"On me," Lindsey tells him with a wink. "Reciprocation," she says and walks away.

"What is *that* about?" Phil asks.

Aaron cannot stop the grin inching across his face, the flush of blood to his cheeks.

"Uh oh," Mora says in a playful manner. "Are we going to have to impeach you?"

"Stop," Aaron tells her. He glances over and yes, there is no jealousy.

"She's very pretty," she tells him.

Aaron grunts and turns away. He picks up the flute, finishes his drink. He wishes he could wave down the server for something stronger but no –

Mora nudges him. "I need a cigarette. Coming with?" she asks Diane across the table.

Diane shakes her head.

Mora frowns in surprise. "Well, okay." She stands. "You alright?"

"I just don't feel like going outside."

"Okay, okay." Mora holds her hands up as she walks away.

"*Are* you okay?" Phil asks Diane moments later.

"Yes. No." She closes her eyes. "Vincent is so brave." Her words are almost a whisper. She opens her eyes and looks at Aaron. "I am glad he's dead. He's got peace now." She takes a breath. "You know instead of impeaching you, I think we should boot her."

"Mora?" Aaron asks.

"She's not going to kill herself."

"What's with you?"

"Last month I was having a really hard time. She came over and you know what she brought? Daisies. A freaking bouquet. If she really wanted to make me to feel better, she would've brought sleeping pills."

"She isn't even sure you wanna kill yourself."

"Why would she think that?"

"Because you said at the first meeting that you either wanted to kill yourself or not live the way you're living. She's hoping that you'll find your own way. She cares –"

"That's the problem. I'm not sure she's trying to help us die. She's probably planning your wedding right now."

Aaron sighs.

When Mora returns, he stands, allows her entrance.

Settling back in, she asks, "Miss anything?"

Silence. Averted eyes.

"Guess I did." She shrugs and reaches for the untouched platter of wings. "This was really sweet of her." She offers one to Aaron. "Maybe you'll just resign?"

Aaron looks at Mora, considers her. *She's not trying to help us die.* His fingers begin to drum the time passing. He wants to say something but he isn't sure what. He just doesn't know.

Balls

by Stephen V. Ramey

My eyes are watching *Modern Family* on ABC, but my brain won't stop obsessing. Tomorrow I'm scheduled to have my balls cut off.

Anne sits knees up in her chair, the cat squeezed beside her. If anything, she looks happy. *It's the least expensive, most effective treatment for your stage of the disease.* That's what the doctor said. He's a urologist straight out of the Marty Feldman school of character acting, bulging eyes, a tendency to extend one finger while he reads from his menu of results, as if preparing for a proctology exam. Dr. Schmitz. I think they added the 'm' when his family arrived on Ellis Island.

"I'm off to bed," Anne says. She stands and strolls through the archway from the living room to the kitchen. I watch her move dishes from the counter to the sink.

Mystery hops down from the chair, wobbly on her eighteen-year-old cat legs. Still, she manages to climb the stairs each night when Anne goes to bed. I wish she would stay with me tonight, a neutered cat, a soon-to-be-neutered man commiserating on his final night intact. Of course she probably does not understand. Nobody understands, not even my comedian friend Jimmy. *Hey, man, you should be happy. Now it won't hurt when Anne's got your testicles in a vice.*

I told him I'm worried about libido, and all he could

83

come back with was that tired joke about the guy who has hand surgery and asks his doctor whether he'll be able to play the piano. I'm about to be emasculated. It's not funny, damn it, it's not.

Anne wipes her hands on a dishtowel and tosses it on the counter. She returns from the kitchen, yawning. "Don't forget to wash that pan before you come to bed."

I start to nod, then stop myself and click the mute button on the remote. "I'm scared," I say in a flat voice. A commercial flashes, a silver car speeding.

Anne's stoicism falters. Her shoulders slump. I think of quicksand sucking a villain down.

"It'll be okay," she says. "I'll be there for you." She smiles bravely, but I can only see sadness in her eyes. "I know this is difficult," she says. "Life isn't fair, but we do the best we –"

"I won't be able to … to …" I try to focus, but her features blur.

Anne pats my shoulder. "Of course you will. Is that what's worrying you?"

Is that all? I shrug away from her hand.

I press the mute button. Sitcom laughter floods the room.

"We'll get through this," Anne says. "You and me, together, always and forever." That was part of our wedding vows. It sounds childish now.

"Do you want me to stay up a while?" She sits on the chair arm and leans toward me. Her breast squishes against my shoulder.

I nudge her away. "Go to bed, Anne. You have a long day tomorrow." After my outpatient surgery, she has three meetings if I remember right.

"If you're sure." She gives me a sideways glance that tells me she's available if I want her.

"Go ahead," I say. "I'm just having a little whine."

She chuckles at that. "I'll give you a rain check, then."

84

"Sure."

Anne squeezes my hand and strolls toward the stairway, Mystery in tow. I watch her hips move. She belly-danced for me once when we were dating. It made me hard. I kind of wish she would do that now, only I know it wouldn't matter. Sex is the last thing I want tonight.

I watch television until the creaking floor tells me Anne is in bed. Then I turn the television off, go to the door, and pull my jacket from the rack. I need to walk off this anxiety.

The night is clear, one of those evenings when you can look up into the stars and know how small you are. The waning half-moon hangs to the south. Growing up in the sixties, I once believed I would go there before I died, dust coating my boots, gravity barely tugging. I used to dream of gliding over a cratered plain, thinking how wonderful it was to be alive. Of course, I also dreamed of falling, the fear boiling up inside me until I snapped awake in bed.

A car crunches past with a boom box throb. A hint of cannabis drifts. The windows are tinted, but must be cracked open. I swallow thickly and consider waving my arms. I would give my last dollar for a joint right now.

The car pauses at the stop sign at the end of our street and turns. By the time I reach the intersection, it's gone. *Where to now?* I think.

I see the history museum where Anne sometimes volunteers, a 1900's era mansion a few hundred yards up the hill. I know the security code. I know where the spare key is hidden. I can go there.

Squeeeeeeee ...

I punch a sequence into the alarm pad, only now

thinking that maybe they've changed the code since I saw Anne use it. Won't *that* be embarrassing.

A life-affirming series of beeps sounds. Silence descends. *Success.*

The house is dark, but for the red blinks of motion sensors. I look up the staircase. There are no sensors on the third floor, where restoration is ongoing. It's peaceful there.

By the time I climb all the flights to the third floor – high ceilings make for long staircases – I'm breathing hard. I can't help thinking that the spot on my lung has grown into full-fledged cancer, and the shortness of breath is the first gasp of my dying.

No, you're just out of shape, Anne's voice assures me. What would she think of me coming here? She could get into hot water with the Historical Society. Why do I do these things?

I don't turn around and march down the stairs. I don't even slow, really, but continue around a corner, using my palms to guide me in the dark. I come to a door and open it.

Moonlight filters through squat windows. The ceiling is not so high here, but the room is large, half the house's width and most of its length. Piles of wood and drywall break up the floor space. Sawhorses stand beneath the largest window. Carpenters have been ripping out interior walls. I remember Anne telling me this used to be a ballroom. Society people would gather here to dance and talk after long days of rigging account books, or bossing mill hunks around. If I stand very still, I can hear the music, the voices, the churning of skirts against stays. A flowery smell wafts. *Perfume.*

And then I see it; the shadows of saw horses and two-by-fours become people, men wearing topcoats, women in lace-trimmed blouses. They move past, bowing, nodding, arm-in-arm like couples carved on a music box.

I slink down until I'm sitting on the floor, back pressed

86

to the wall, sanity slipping. It's not enough I have cancer, not enough they want to castrate me ... I hug my knees.

"Get up, silly." The voice is both real and unreal, the memory of a dream.

A young woman reaches down, wrist bent. Her dress is frilled, and floor length. I recognize her face in the moonlight. It's Amanda the resident ghost – according to volunteers who have heard her or felt her touch. Her portrait hangs downstairs.

"Dance with me," Amanda says. She has a pretty smile, a smooth complexion. Her hair is cut short. This must be before she married the embezzler who built a boat too large to get through the workshop door.

I take her hand. It's solid, warm. We join the mannequin flow. I've never danced, yet this waltz comes naturally. The music ebbs, and I see a string quartet in the corner. A man saws at a cello, his eyes like black marbles.

This is ludicrous. I stop. Amanda's fingers pull from mine like taffy. Another man takes my place, and she continues dancing.

I part a set of pocket doors. The rollers run smoothly, which seems wrong. There's another room on the other side, a billiard table. A man leans over one end, petite cue stick propped between knuckles. I smell sweet tobacco.

"Shall we make it interesting, Jameson?" This from a fat man by the wall. A pipe smolders from his hand.

"Indeed, sir," the first man says. "I welcome your green."

"A ten that you cannot sink the seven ball into the corner," the fat mans says.

"Done," the other says, and strokes through his shot. I wince as balls crack. The seven ricochets past the cup and back toward me.

The shooter stands. "It must be the table, or the floor."

The fat man laughs. "Something is always crooked with you, eh, Greer?" He looks directly at me. "Do you play, sir?"

"Me?" My voice echoes too loudly. The balls disappear, the men, the table, the music in my ears. Everything. I'm suddenly alone, back pressed to the wall, eyes staring past shadow scaffoldings of wood, to the waning moon. Even the moon is not constant.

Amanda whispers from deep within my head: "You know that you can't go back, Stephen, you can never return." And I do know it. Maybe I've known it all along.

The Stranger

by Gay Degani

Five long months have passed since he'd trudged along the Old Road back to his car against a ninety-mile-an-hour wind, eyes watering, ears ringing, his unzipped sweatshirt snapping behind him. He'd collapsed into the driver's seat and shoved his hand into his pants while the storm's fury rattled around him. He was gone before the oak tree fell on Jamie's bungalow.

He never forgets the ferocious wind that blew down from the north, the clear black sky, the brilliance of scrubbed air, the sharp cold in his chest when he breathed. He hasn't forgotten the sting of windburn on his cheeks as he lay in his own bed. And Jamie's silhouette in the window, dark against the glowing yellow of her living room, haunts him when he brushes his teeth, when he sits alone in his office at the community college, when he slams his car door and watches his daughter dash out down the front steps to greet him.

He's yearned more for Jamie than anyone before, delaying the endgame longer, embracing the task of waiting. He's kept her on the edge of his mind, his pleasure in the denial of his urges, that tension created by his unfulfilled physical need. He's survived on his mental projection of possibilities, refusing to give in. It's this discipline that is his most exquisite torture.

He finally returns to the Old Road after his grades are turned in and his wife and daughter are halfway across the continent visiting his in-laws. He parks the car in the same place as before, but decides on one more excruciating delay before yielding to his bliss. Instead of jogging along the asphalt as he'd done in January, he scrambles down a path into the arroyo where the late afternoon sun haloes the leaves of trees and glints off the thread of water at the bottom of a concrete channel. He's never gone this long before without giving up, giving in, ruining something that could have been perfect. His heart bangs against his ribs, his body buzzes in anticipation as he struts along the chain-link. In this wildish place on the edge of town, in its golden light, he prepares himself for his final move.

Dust kicks up under his feet as he marvels at his own restraint, how he's managed to stay away so long. Jamie's face comes to him, clear and sharp, tongue pressed against her front teeth, her hazel eyes wary, standing in his classroom, handing in her late assignment, her voice low and throaty, making her excuses. She isn't beautiful, merely pretty – and sad. He lusts for sad. And she isn't coy, never flirting with him, but he knows she's holding back, as disciplined as he, kindred spirits. He allows himself to imagine his finger tracing a line from her mouth, down along her nipples, first one, then the other, slowly to her cunt. His own body answers, his mind a remarkable instrument of persuasive creation.

A twist to his ankle shakes him out of his reverie and tumbles him against something rough and hard, scraping his hand as he tries to catch his fall. He looks up and gapes because his brain can't sort what he sees: a knot of snakes bristling from a giant head in the weeds along the path, its Medusa shadow stretching behind, his own shadow leaping away. It takes him a moment to recognize the stump of a tree, torn from the ground and abandoned on its side, its snakes nothing but curling roots.

He tries to laugh at himself, but the sound is forced, bitter. He spits out "Fool. Idiot. Jerk-off!" and kicks at the mocking stump, missing, and wheeling around, stomps away, up the path to the Old Road.

All these months, he's taken pleasure in denying himself, thinking of her as he watched his female students waiting in the hall before class, brushing past them without quite touching, venturing down the rows of desks while he lectured, standing close enough to feel their heat, but never more than that. Medusa, ravished by Poseidon in the temple of Athena.

Time for him to do his own ravishing.

The sun slants cool and low behind him, yet sweat beads his forehead. At the top, on the verge, he forces himself to lean over, catch his breath, and prolongs his moment of perfect anticipation until a shudder of need forces him to look up.

"No." He closes his eyes.

Opens them. "No."

On the night of the windstorm, Jamie stood in the window of a bungalow across the Old Road, but now, there's no woman in the window. There's no window, no bungalow. Only a crumbling brick foundation remains.

How did this happen? He crosses the road and studies the yard. Then he knows. Five hundred trees in the city had been uprooted by the windstorm. Next to where the bungalow used to stand, hidden behind a hedge, he sees another Medusa, another tree stump yanked on its side, its mass of roots facing away from him, a couple small stacks of cut oak nearby. He sways a little remembering that wind, what it had given him, the storm, the woman, the discipline. And then took away. He'd denied himself because of the rules, *his* rules. And he'd lasted five months because then, everything would be in place. She would be ready. He would be ready. And the endgame was always worth it.

But all those months to gape at a hole in the ground? He moves a hand to his crotch, fingers himself through the cloth of his pants, then gives up. This isn't how the game is played.

In the Dark

by Sally-Anne Macomber

To: Milton Flaxmill, Red Cow Publishing
From: Trudy Polaris
Date: June 20, 2014 12:07 a.m.
Re: Getting it right

Hi Milton,

I am completely in the dark at the moment. I am also munching cheese as I type, so now I have an excuse for all my typos!!

The tax break my husband has us on here is not proving as financially successful as we had hoped so I am sitting in my skiing gear – thermal extend-a-bra, padded ski pants, a beanie with an insulated pom-pom on my head – in the secret basement of our Tyrolean hideaway, hoping the Eurozone tax agents and the Tyrolean Electricity Commission and maybe a dairy farmer or two (who might still bear a grudge about that silly Bulgarian fetta escapade) will get the hint and leave us alone.

We have no money to pay them.

All we have is our talent and determination and a little fetta we are able to chip off the great wall of the stuff still sitting in the garden, which we do at night, with a serrated cheese knife, when all the watchers and spies and observationists have gone home. Which is after the sun goes down, so about 10:00pm or so here, now it's June.

Plus of course, I also have this email lifeline to you and *Nuclear Fission in The Pyrénées* which I am secretly hoping will prove to be the masterpiece we all deserve it to be, and which will earn me big dollars and get us out of this tax crevasse we're in.

But, Milton *mein Liebling* … on to more important things …

I have been playing around with fonts and am wondering if there is room in *Nuclear Fission in The Pyrénées* for a few of them. What do you think?

I was originally thinking about 20.

I was online – there is little else to do here in this basement, even though the sun is shining and summer is well on its way outside (when do I get to go outside though, I ask you, and feel the sun's warmth on my face and shed the thermal extend-a-bra, padded ski pants, and beanie with the insulated pom-pom on my head? I mean, I ask you, just when?!) – and I came across a free font site. (And not a font-free site, which is a very different thing!)

There are some amazing fonts out there! My God, so many! It makes my head spin to think of the design opportunities we are missing out on by not using as many beautiful fonts as we can.

So I have changed my mind and am now wondering if we could have a different font on every page?

This would mean we could also have different style fonts for each different chapter. We could have 1920's style fonts for *Above and Beyond Andorra* ('Gonggong Sans' is a firm favourite for this chapter, the serifs are so clean and brutal in that Deco way I love) and 1950's fonts for *Nuts in the Nuclear Age*. (Can't decide if 'Extraordinary Nevada Tahoe Marie Extra Bold Light' would be better starting off this chapter, or 'Mud Italic'. 'Mud Italic' is sort of woodsy in a Lincoln Logs hunting lodge kind of way, while 'Extraordinary Nevada Tahoe Marie Extra Bold Light' has a more streamlined Jet Age soda pop at the drive-in in an old Chevy feel.)

I want the title pages to all have the same font though – more seems a little indulgent, and I like the idea of the calm before the storm, before the fonts get completely frenzied – so I'm thinking maybe 'New Verity Nadir' is the best choice for the title pages. There's a bold-faced, bald clean clear truth to 'New Verity Nadir' that I think strikes at the heart of what *Nuclear Fission in The Pyrénées* is really all about.

Unfortunately, it's also a very small size font, so an appropriate size might be 1514 or pretty close to that.

And given the theme of the book, I've decided the title pages would work best in black, with the letters in white. So I have added the title in 'New Verity Nadir' below, size 462, white letters on black background, just so you can see it for yourself. You might need to make it bigger so you can see it properly. If you scroll your cursor (or curser? or cursur?) across the box below, you will see just what I mean.

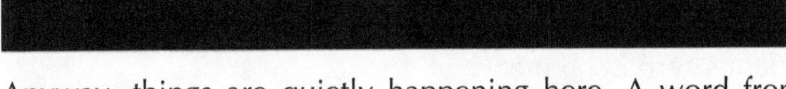

Anyway, things are quietly happening here. A word from you now and then would be good, though. I like to feel connected.

Your writer gal-pal,

Trudy

Cobwebs

by Mandy Nicol

Mum doesn't want me to go out tonight because she thinks I met Charlie online. She thinks I'm being foolhardy. I've given up explaining that I met him at Angela's barbecue, that we've been keeping in touch by email, that I've had coffee with him a couple of times when I've driven to Melbourne to fit Angela's wedding dress. Angela's free wedding dress. The one I'm now glad my sister twisted my arm to make. Charlie hasn't kidnapped or murdered or fleeced me yet but Mum won't be convinced.

"Did you put hairspray in your bag?" she asks.

"What's the matter with my hair?" I pat my head, though I'm not sure what that can tell me.

"Not for your hair, Nadia. For an emergency. It'll work like capsicum spray if you get him in the eyes."

"For God's sake, Mum."

The exasperation in my voice stirs the dogs. Old Peregrine's kind eyes and Seph's bright and beady little buttons zero in on me.

"Just put a can in your bag, will you please?" asks Mum. "Better to be safe than sorry."

I go to my bedroom, pick up the hairspray from on top of my dressing table and toss it in a drawer – I figure she'll check. I look at my face in the mirror and that's a mistake because I look like a sad clown with those downturned glossy red lips. I hope it's the Mum effect, I hope I don't always look this sour.

And now I panic. What the hell am I doing? Having coffee is one thing but this is a date. A real date. He's driving over two hundred kilometres just to take me out to dinner. And he'll already be well on the way so I can't ring his mobile and say I've changed my mind. I don't know where he's staying, or even if he's staying. God I hope he doesn't think he's staying here. Why didn't I ask him?

I count the charms on my bracelet, make sure there are seven. Then I count them again. Yes, seven. I make sure the lucky horseshoe is there, which of course it is, because I've counted seven. Twice.

This is going to be so awkward. How are you supposed to act on a first date when you're thirty-four years old? Why didn't I think things through instead of jumping in and gushing *yes* as soon as he asked? We were outside a café in Carlton, saying goodbye, it was a casual invitation, I could so easily have said *thanks but no*. Why didn't I say no?

I flop back onto my bed and kick off the tottery heels. Why did I think me tottering around on high heels would be a good look?

I stare at the cobweb on the ceiling. I can't see a spider anywhere, never have, yet there's always a cobweb in the corner. I contemplate the invisible spider and gradually my heart stops banging around in my chest.

I lie on my bed for a long time. Until I hear tyres on the gravel outside, then a car door slams. I stand up, smooth down my dress, spray some perfume on my neck. I bend down to gather my shoes and I picture Charlie being greeted at the front door by Mum and a can of flyspray.

I scoot to the door barefooted.

To the Dogs

by Margaret Bingel

Jersey's Cats, Dogs, and Other Strays is always open early on Sundays because, being at the junction of three churches and a synagogue, when the faithful go and hear about God's love, their hearts tug either towards feeding the homeless, or adopting a pet. There are always volunteers to open early, so scheduling one or two to show up at 5:00am to greet prospective owners is never a problem. Reggie, the animal shelter's director for three years, loves taking the early morning Sunday shift regardless of his other volunteers' availability. He loves the looks the tired and world-weary give the animals on their way to worship, and the joy that spreads across their face when they take one of them home.

Reggie flips the sign to 'Open' and makes his rounds. Feedings, belly rubs, and investigating wounds on some of the new arrivals keep him busy for an hour. Strays often show up with more cuts than he likes, but he and the other volunteers always make sure the animals' needs are taken care of. After opening the door to the free play area, he watches the cats and dogs run out and start mauling the ropes and toys scattered on the floor.

With the animals playing, he hears the door chime and sees Sylvia, Karl, Meagan, and Sam walk in, talking about the end of the school year. Karl holds a cardboard jug of coffee, and Sylvia has a paper bag full of cups and stirrers.

Reggie follows them into the kitchen.

"I'm thinking 'beach' tomorrow, who's in?" Meagan asks. "We need to have some fucking fun, Jesus Christ."

"Oh my gosh, Meagan, watch your mouth, geez." Sylvia is always uncomfortable with Meagan's swearing. "Kids could be here."

"But they're not!" Meagan grabs a creamer. "I'm going to enjoy this cup of joe with Joe."

Sam rolls his eyes. He thinks Meagan spends way too much time on just a few of "her pets" as she selfishly puts it. He prefers to handle the snakes, one of the few who can stomach feeding them. (He keeps a boa at home.) It's not that he doesn't like Meagan, he just thinks she's unaware of anything that isn't cute and isn't her.

Around 8:00, everyone hears the door chime. Glancing about, Karl, not playing with any of the cats, steps out to greet the customer.

"Hi, welcome to Jersey's, may I help you?" he asks Ned.

Ned squints his eyes at the teenager. "I'm looking for a dog." He has been dreaming about one for months.

Ned follows Karl to the play area. Ned walks right in and stares at all the animals, chewing on toys, sleeping in corners.

"Feel free to walk around," Karl says with a touch of sarcasm. "Let them sniff you first, then you'll see if they like you."

Ned feels a humming under his skin. So many dogs! How will he every find the right one? He watches what looks like a pug sniff the ass of a chihuahua. He chuckles, but isn't interested. The animals are not what they seem, he thinks. They are waiting for someone. They are waiting to choose.

Suddenly, a cold, wet thing touches his hand. Jerking away, Ned looks down and sees a dog, sniffing him. Smaller than a medium-sized dog, she looks up at Ned with mournful eyes. He's locked in her gaze. The bitch wags her tail and pants, her mouth looking like a smile.

"What can you tell me about this one?" Ned asks Karl, reaching down to pet her. She sniffs his hand again, nuzzling his palm.

"That bitch?" Karl smirks. "She's some kind of beagle, we think. Nothing wrong with her, but she hates everyone. Howls at the kids when they come to pet her. I think she's yours."

Scratching her ears, Ned agrees.

"Her name is Nadia," Karl says, "and she's a runaway. Her owners have never claimed her. She's been here for two years, waiting for someone to let her guard down around."

But Ned isn't listening. He stops scratching Nadia's ears and she whines. When he looks down, he sees he's forgotten to tie his shoes, again.

A Frankenstein Storm

by Darryl Price

It's been storming something terrible all day today, hitting the windows like relentless sopping wet sheets. It's not scary. Just very, very lonely sounding, if you know what I mean. Monotonous, feels like I'm on a bed on a large boat of some heavy kind, or in a tub boat lost out to sea. There's one for you, Doc. Consider that a freebie.

Sometimes when I lie awake in bed at night I wonder about all those lives out there being lived among the so many beautiful lights. Someone once described them to me as being like campfires. I wanted nothing more in my life than to sit around those campfires and be part of that circle of knowing. But it seems I mostly lived my life in fast cars. Going places or returning from them. I've never felt warm or invited in this world, except the once, and as you know that didn't turn out so well for me.

It's not her fault. I swear. It's nobody's fault. It's just a bad wind came and blew my whole life down to the ground and I've been having a hell of a time ever since trying to pick up all the little scattered pieces. Sometimes I don't even know where to begin. I start and stop a lot. I used to keep a diary, but it was all stupid shit you know, pardon my English, Doc, like someone trying to write someone a folk song and failing at it miserably. It just didn't make any real sense to anyone else but me. Well. Me and her. She always seemed to get it.

I guess that's what I'm doing here, right? Beginning, or trying to begin. You guys are making a Frankenstein monster out of me! I'm only going to frighten little children, or myself if I look in the mirror. What I need is a sad soul hospital. You got any of those lying around? That's where it hurts the most. How you gonna fix that? I'm broke on the inside of my feelings.

Ok, I know you said I could write down whatever I wanted to, but I'm still trying to come up with those bizarre little mythological stories for you, since you seem to like those the best out of all of them. If it's proof that you want that I'm as sane as the next guy who's down on his luck, well, I don't know how to give you that, except to say that I believe it about myself, even if no one else does right now. And the reason I say that is everyone here looks at me strangely. What I wouldn't give for one kind look that doesn't come from anyplace but itself.

Would I even think like that if I were crazy?

Here's your story, now leave me alone: once there was a princess who could talk to butterflies. The only problem was that the butterflies never really had too much to say back to her, really, and so she never learned a lot about what they were thinking. One day she was sitting on the grass when a tiny little blue thing fluttered around her knees. Hey, she said, I want to ask you a question! The butterfly landed on her arm and looked up at her enormous head. Do you know where I can find some juicy red roses, he said. No, well, yes, I guess I do, but first you have to answer me a few questions, then I'll tell you. Oh I really don't have time for all this, the butterfly said. Oh but please, said the Princess in a great sobbing voice and so the butterfly agreed. You may ask only 2 questions, and then I really must be going. Alright she said. First what is the meaning of butterflies, and secondly, do you believe there is a god? The butterfly pumped his little wings up and down and said, the meaning of butterflies is really very simple, we mean whatever you think we mean, and as for god, we feel glad enough to be here in the modern world with the rest of you. But those aren't real answers, said the princess. You're just saying whatever comes into your mind so I'll show you to those roses. Oh very well said the butterfly. Butterflies mean all life is lived in a pretty good circle and god is whatever we put in that circle as we fly through our days together. Hmmm, said the Princess, I suppose that will have to do. It's better than the first answers you gave me. She gave the butterfly directions to the rose bush that grew on the other side of her house, but when he took off he actually went the other way instead.

Well I'm tired now, Doc. I'm going to knock it all off for the night. Hopefully by morning the bolts in my neck will be fully charged and I'll be able to walk out of here on my own two glued-together feet.

Good night.

Flying Solo

by Teresa Burns Gunther

It's a Tuesday evening and a busy week at work. But, restless at home, with nothing for dinner Rachel goes for a drive and finds herself standing at Sea Cliff on the rim of the Pacific staring out across its unknowable expanse to Japan. She always avoids the places tourists congregate but it's twenty-eight minutes before sunset and the sky is going wild and Sutro's at The Cliff House offers a view with benefits.

It's a quiet night and the host has a table for two by the window. Rachel orders a drink aware of her singularity, wondering if she'll always be a one: Table for one, single occupant, travelling alone. No one else is flying solo at Sutro's.

A middle-aged couple leans in at each other, eyes narrowed, mouths moving with words that look sharp, unhappiness for dinner.

At a table near the bus station a freckled woman cuts her children's food and mops up spilled milk. She talks, her smile feigning happiness while her husband ogles a duo of twenty-somethings, blonde and brunette, laughing and fluffing their hair, at a table one over.

Left of the sirens' table a balding businessman in a dark and tired suit is oblivious to their appeal and the blushing sunset. His square chin is lifted in a pose of amused disinterest at what is clearly a negative assessment coming at him from a large man opposite, a clearly dissatisfied customer gesticulating, complaints issuing from a florid face with drops of spit lit by the sinking sun.

A white-collared priest dines with an elderly couple in the corner. He sermonizes as he eats, oblivious of the woman wincing, her eyes darting away from the views of his masticated dinner in his too full mouth.

A pimply busboy leans against the wall watching the tables with eyes that see nothing; his mind gone travelling somewhere his body longs to follow.

Rachel thanks the waiter for the glass of scotch delivered neat with a coaster. She breathes in its peaty aroma and the thrill of a rare San Francisco June evening, fogless, still warm at 8:03 pm! She slips off her shoes, puts her feet on the other chair, empty and waiting to hold them. She drinks alone in a summer dress as the sun lingers inches above the horizon, fracturing the sky in a Hallelujah chorus of colors, ecstatic striations of gold and crimson that reach up across the sky, spill over the waving surface of the sea, and paint her white tablecloth pink as the noise of restaurant life becomes a cushioning hum.

Morgana Malone and the Miracle of Christmas

by Matt Potter

"Be holding this," Ludmilla says, and pushes a samovar into my arms.

The samovar is big and silver and crushes against my breastbone because it weighs a ton. (Or tonne, if you want to be metric about it. Or actually, 1.016 tons, if you want to be *accurate* and metric although it could be the other way around. Not that I adore the Imperial measurement system but since I lost my job at Grigor's therapy practice and don't have a lot of money and spend a lot of time alone at home, I'm on the internet quite often. And I found a website just the other day comparing metric to Imperial and it was *mesmerising*.)

Meanwhile, Ludmilla is busy piling things up on the kitchen bench. What looks like a pasta press. Then what she said is an exotic blini maker. (She didn't say *exotic*, I did, or thought it when she lugged it inside – 'gee, that looks exotic,' I thought – and she saw me looking at it and said, "No peeking – it makes blinis.") Then her famous borscht pot. And then another pot she's using to make 'sochivo' (aka 'kutia', just depends upon which part of Russia you come from. Although I think Ludmilla is not from Russia but is an ethnic Russian from the Ukraine or maybe even Georgia, it's hard to work out just where she's from because when she's talking about her childhood she gets excited and spits a lot.)

Thinking of Ludmilla spitting makes me think of sweet Mr Rubinstein, who would come in every day for therapy. Or as he'd say, "because I am enjoying some chillink here in the waiting room." Mr Rubinstein of the eye patch and the toupée, who loved the widening grey-brown strip on my head. (I am growing out the orange I had it dyed because (1) I really don't like looking like a carrot and (2) I can't afford to get it dyed orange again by a professional hairdresser.)

My mind whips back to 'sochivo' or 'kutia', the special dish of boiled wheat sweetened with honey and sometimes dried fruit, which I know about because I looked it up on the internet. Ludmilla emailed me the links. She said it would be a nice gesture of international goodwill if I made it for the dinner party tonight, especially because I'm not Russian. "And I know you are not Russian," she said, "because no Russians are having orange hair."

(But I've never been that good at boiling wheat! So I'm going to pay her to boil the wheat instead. Or, give her a big discount on her first month's rent. Apparently making 'sochivo' can take hours.)

"What is your matter?" Ludmilla glares at me. "Your eyes are spinning spinning spinning inside your head and your brain is looking like it is cooking."

The samovar, I realise, with its cute green filigreed frog bobbling on the very top, almost touching my nostrils, is crushing the life out of me but there is no free space on any of the kitchen benches or the table to put it down and it's too magnificent and ornate and curlicued (and heavy and awkward) to put it down on the floor so I lean against the wall still clutching it but actually, it's the pantry door I'm leaning against and then I realise almost immediately as Ludmilla makes a beeline for me that I'm in her way.

"You are standing where I need to going," Ludmilla says. "Salt, salt, I need salt!"

I sort of lob out of her way – or shuffle, really, with the samovar in my arms – and then I realise I don't have any salt anyway. Because I never have salt.

"I don't have any salt, Ludmilla," I say, as she pulls the pantry door open and the 15-month calendar – January 2013 to March 2014 – smacks against the back of the door. "Remember last week when you were here, you had to use sugar because I didn't have any salt?"

Ludmilla stops in her tracks. "No salt?! You have … no … salt?!"

"No," I say, "I don't really cook with salt."

"No salt?!"

"No," I repeat. "No salt." Although, really, I'm not cooking with anything at the moment because I'm not really cooking because I'm not really eating.

Ludmilla closes the pantry door. "Then lucky lucky lucky you for I am moving in with you," she says. "So I know now why you be so skinny." And she stretches it out, *skee-ee-nee*, like I'm suddenly a lot taller too.

Although, if anything, if you looked at me – *really* looked at me – you'd say I was shorter.

"Where can I put this samovar, Ludmilla? It's pulling my arms out of their sockets."

"And lucky lucky lucky you our first meal together is for Christmas in July in June," she says. She steps over to the sink and looks through the window at the grey early winter sky. "No rain," she adds. "There is winter but there is no rain."

"Could you clear a spot on the bench?" I say, waddling over to the sink. This samovar is really killing me but if I drop it, it's going to dent the floor. Which is concrete but probably the dentable kind.

"But Christmas in July in June with *no salt*?" she says, turning to scowl at me, her mouth a frown and a smile at the same time, so really, just skewed. "Im – pos – si – ble!" she says, like she's just discovered the word and she's trying it out. "Impossible, impossible." She picks up her battered blue vinyl handbag from its perch on top of the exotic blini maker and slings it into the crook of her elbow. "*No* salt, *no* Christmas in July in June. So we buy salt."

The samovar rattles on the back seat as I drive Ludmilla in my faded watermelon pink Nissan Micra to the nearest supermarket. Ludmilla's first gesture as my new housemate is this Christmas in July party except it's not July yet, it's June, but it *is* the 25th. Accepting this party is my first housematerly act of diplomacy.

("Then we can be celebrating the big Australian tradition, Christmas in July," Ludmilla had said, when she told me it would be a good idea if I got a housemate. Like her. And soon. Like next week (which is actually this week now). When she came to my house to give me a free salt reading. At her own instigation. Except, of course, I didn't have any salt.

"But we don't do Christmas in July here," I'd said, licking the rolling pin before running it across the sugar I'd spread across the kitchen table. "Some of us barely do Christmas in December. We're just going through the motions 'til we can go to the beach for the summer holidays."

Taking the rolling pin from my grasp, she'd glanced at the sugar impressions made on the wood, then looked me up and down, raised an eyebrow, and harrumphed.

"And it won't even be July next week," I'd added, "it'll still be June."

"Christmas in July *in June*," she'd said. "I bring my samovar and we celebrate *big* Australian Christmas in July in June tradition.")

109

§

Ludmilla opens the passenger door and slings the 10-kilo bag of salt on the floor in front of the seat. Then, "What is this?" she says, and picks up the white envelope she was sitting on as we drove to the supermarket.

She holds it closer to read it, her thin lips mouthing my name on the front.

"It's from Grigor," I say. "That's his writing."

"Ach, but he writes not like a Russian," Ludmilla says.

"He's not Russian," I say. "His real last name is Smith."

"He writes not like a Russian," she repeats.

"Yes, his real last name is Smith," I say again. And then, before we go another round of *he writes not like a Russian / his real last name is Smith*, "I've been meaning to open it all week," I say. "It's just been lying there on the seat. I came out one morning and found it stuck to the windscreen."

Doors slam and I turn the key in the ignition. Just as I steer the faded Nissan Micra right, out of the car park, I hear ripping paper and turn to catch Ludmilla opening the letter.

"*As you have ruined my life and made a mockery of my wedding*," she reads. (Then to me but more to herself, "Who is this *mockery*?" she snorts.) "*Here is the bill for my ruination*." And then to herself but more to me, "There is a lot of serious numbers."

The samovar skids across the backseat as I pull over to the kerb, and right foot on the brake and with the engine still running, take the letter from her hand. My eyes run down the accompanying page of numbers. It's an itemised account of everything spent (and not paid for, by the look of things) for his wedding. The schnoodle, the platinum wedding rings, Grigor's rhinoplatsy, the vegan wedding bouquets ... oh, everything.

So did Grigor marry Zebadie or was *that* passed on to someone else too?

"But this is *verrry* Russian thing," Ludmilla pronounces, her chin nodding. "What is *yacht*?" she says, but she says it like it's spelled, 'y-a-ch-t'.

I shake my head. Can he come after me for the money?

Ludmilla rips the letter from my hand. "Look," she points at the bill, "you know bad people, bad people be advantaged over you. So get rid of bad people."

I pull on the handbrake, turn the key and the engine shudders to a stop.

"Christmas in July in June is here," Ludmilla says. "Maybe you meet a nice *real* Russian man."

I look out the driver's window. It's not raining but everything is a watery blur.

"Okay, your friend Ludmilla, I help you. I cook you 'sochivo'," she adds, "for free. Okay?"

I turn to see her peering at me. And, smiling so her beige teeth show past her thin lips, she pats my knee.

I twist and look at the backseat, at the silver samovar resting between two seatbelt buckles. And wonder who should I smash over the head with it first: Grigor, or Ludmilla?

Nichole

by Gary Percesepe

O Sara!

It's June 26th and this date always reminds me of a woman I once knew. She lives in Brooklyn now, not far from you. I'd take you both to lunch when I'm in town next week, but I don't know how to reach her, how to find her. She's in Brooklyn, somewhere. I miss her. I miss her today.

I'd see Nichole once a week at the small literary magazine where we worked. The magazine had a good reputation. Thousands of hopeful writers sent their short stories to a post office box downtown. Nichole logged them in. The managing editor scanned the pile for names she recognized – writers we'd published previously, like T.C. Boyle, James Purdy, Gordon Lish – and for "agented work". The rest was slush. The slush was stood upright in two large boxes in the far corner of the magazine's one room office. There it would sit until one of the "readers" would take home a pile. Nichole and I were readers.

One day I read a story that knocked me out. The author had no credits. Straight from the slush, wrapped in a plain brown envelope, the story was about two lonely and alienated teenaged kids who are surprised one morning to find each other. A story I'd heard a thousand times. But it was the way the story was told – full of feeling, accurate, without a trace of condescension, right as rain. It filled the heart. I called Nichole.

We made a picnic in the park. I read the story out loud. Toward the end, the boy and girl meet at the high school, at first light. There is the sound of a lawn mower in the middle distance, and the smell of fresh cut grass. They are seated in silence on the steps of the school. The girl raises her shirt.

I finished reading. There was silence for the space of a minute. Then Nichole took off her shirt. She kissed me. "Shirt-raising fiction," she said.

I know, I know – you're smiling at that. Ha.

Wait a sec – there's someone at the door.

OK, I'm back. Delivery guy. Galleys for my story collection. So, anyway –

We fucked that day, outside at a state park, in a lovely meadow by a statue (oh so phallic) and we shared a bottle of wine and some cheese and crackers I had thought to bring. Or maybe she brought the wine? I don't remember. But I read her that story and then she did what she did with her shirt, and I was like, uh oh, and then – O Sara! – we began to make love and she forgot she had a tampon in and we laughed about that – I mean, really? – and I removed it, or she did and I was inside her, but we both could not stop laughing it was so fucking funny and by then I was thinking I wonder if this is right, I had been affair-less for so long, and I cared about N in all of the right ways, so we just held each other then and went on laughing about the errant tampon, and of course a few weeks later she came out to me, the first person she told, she read it to me from her JOURNAL, the pages she had written after the interview she did with Ani DiFranco and KNEW she was in love, and I was so happy for her, and she told all of this to me in my car, where she went on reading her journal – and she later wrote a poem for her poetry class at Antioch, a poem about making love to an older man who wears a wedding ring, and the poem was, in my memory, the most beautiful poem

I've ever heard, because it came straight from her innocent Italian heart. She said it had shocked her classmates when she had read it aloud in class, and she folded it in half and handed it to me (like a fool, I have somehow lost it). She had a heart-shaped face, and a big smile and a way of looking at you that drew you directly in – that made you feel like you were the only person on earth alive. When she moved to Brooklyn I would get cards from her, not Hallmark cards but these lovely handmade cards with crayon art and multicolored, with little tufts of lace or something glued in – the most creative cards, and every card, every fucking one of them would begin like this:

O Gary!

This is a convention i have adopted, in memory of her

And I learned early on that I could never give her a book to read unless I wanted to GIVE her a book, because that was her rule – she never returned a book, if you gave it to her it was hers – and she explained this to me one day and we laughed at that too – she was a woman with rules.

I gave her a print of a Picasso painting one day, from the blue period, the man with the guitar, and she kept that too – I brought her a big basket of pizzelles one Christmas, for her and her friends, vanilla ones and chocolate that Savannah and I had made – I liked to give her little things.

I bought her a dress one day when I was in Roma. She had wanted to go to Italy with me but then at the last minute she couldn't – I kept expecting her to show up at my room or to run into her at the Pantheon or the Spanish Steps, the whole week I was there. But of course she never showed.

She had, it appears, never worn a dress in her life! Ha! Oh, I loved to see that dress on her, she wore it ONE time, to an Italian lunch restaurant I took her to in Columbus, a place called Bravo! And we talked in Italian and English to the waiters, and I asked her what it was like for her to make love to a woman, to kiss a woman, and we had this funny conversation, the only one of its kind I remember, and it was so funny to see her in that little blue dress, with black leggings I also bought her, to cover her hairy legs, and of course I had bought it for her as a joke.

I wound up writing a poem for her, which I published somewhere or other. Nichole and I were friends, not lovers, and I valued that. I remember thinking at the time: where can I ever find a friend like this?

And then, years later, I met you.

One day I took N to my house and got her up on one of my horses, and we went for a long trail ride together, she on the big black gelding, and I was riding a lovely bay mare, and there were apple trees along our trail and I reached over and plucked an apple off the tree for her and then one for myself, and we rode in silence through the colored woods one fall, with Trouble, the big Irish setter, leading the way, running along ahead of us –

She sat in on some of my classes on friendship love and romance at the conservative college where I taught – and the other girls looked at her as if they were seeing someone from Jupiter – she was dressed in the classic Antioch thrift shop look, and the conservative big-time Christian girls in their plaid skirts and silk blouses and pearls – it was so funny. She couldn't find anyone to hit on, and was a bit disappointed. We were both misplaced souls, and it made us sad sometimes to know how we didn't belong anywhere we went, which is why maybe we went places together –

And the terrible day in November when all hell broke loose with M and the idiot husband who called the house and I thought I would lose my job, my marriage, my family, it was Nichole who first took me into her arms and held me when I thought I would have no life left to live and she said you will go on, you will live, you do not need that place, that ridiculous college, there will be a better one for you, and she was right –

115

I went to her Antioch graduation and saw her parents, and there was N, in a strapless black gown dressed as if going out to dinner in her native Philly, and her hairy armpits displayed to perfection and a string of pearls set against the black dress and her olive skin. I didn't speak to her that day, did not get to see her, stayed away because she was leaving and I couldn't bear to say goodbye to her, so I watched from a distance, and let her go –

Her cards: she would tell me about her love life, the women she was sleeping with, then who she was living with, what concoction she was cooking and the wine (she had little money and HUGE student loans for her Antioch degree in POETRY! – ha! she was the LEAST practical person on earth i have ever met, less practical even than M, which is saying something, as I thought M lived on dreams alone) – and one week I was in NYC and staying at the Chelsea Hotel and I remember Nichole came by to pick me up and we went to an Italian restaurant a block or so away (I MUST find that restaurant again, as I remember it so well, and placed it in another of my short stories, somewhere), and she walked me back to the hotel and we joked about going up but both knew that was a dumb idea and we didn't want it, either of us, though there was a tug when I watched her spin and walk away – but I let her go. Then one day the cards stopped coming –

O Sara!

She is somewhere in Brooklyn.

Can we ever know what we want?

Call me later –

xo

Samford Awakens from a Month-Long Coma

by Nathaniel Tower

Samford flickers his eyes open then snaps them shut, squeezing them tight against the buzzing fluorescent lights.

The last thing he remembers is charging toward the finish line of the One-Mile Run in the Clone Olympics. The crowd was roaring, and he was leading by over 100 meters, easily on his way to a world record.

"Did I win?" he mutters to the empty room. Well, not completely empty. There is plenty of medical equipment.

The lights buzz in response, brightening even through his closed eyelids.

A door pops open. Through small slits Samford watches the blurry figure in a white coat enter. The figure, whom Samford assumes is a doctor, jots notes on a clipboard. At least that's what it looks like.

After standing over Samford for a few minutes, scrawling notes, the doctor says, "And how are you, Samford?"

"Did I win the race?" Samford asks, his voice like gravel.

The doctor continues to write notes. Samford watches him reach for something metallic.

"This will only hurt for a moment." The metal object attaches to Samford's right eyelid and tears it open. Light floods his eye, and Samford thinks his head will explode from the overwhelming brightness. He tries to scream, but the doctor muffles his mouth with a gloved hand.

"It's better if you don't." He reaches for another metal object and places it on Samford's other eye. The pain of rushing light eclipses what he felt when the right eye was forced open.

Samford's body gyrates on the table. Unable to close his eyes, he pounds his legs and arms to tolerate the pain. For the first time since waking up he feels the shackles on his hands and feet.

"It's best that you not do that," the doctor says. He holds a small bottle above Samford's eyes. "If I miss, this could burn your face off."

Samford shakes even more violently at the toxic drops the doctor holds above his eyes.

"You are lucky I have good aim." Samford watches a thick drop release from the bottle and plummet toward his eye. The drop looks enormous as it makes impact, sizzling instantly and distorting everything Samford sees to red. The doctor repeats the process to the other eye.

Samford's vision flashes through the full spectrum of colors before the doctor releases the eye clamps and his eyes fall shut.

"Rest now," the doctor says. "I'll be back in a few hours to answer any questions you have."

The doctor is gone before Samford can force his eyes open again. To his surprise, his vision is clear and he has no more pain. He has no trouble keeping his eyes open either. In fact, he finds it almost impossible to close them, even for the momentary action of blinking.

Once he tires of staring at the lights and the tiny holes in the ceiling (what are those holes for anyway?), he squeezes his eyes closed for more than ten seconds. Of course, as soon as he drifts off to sleep, the door bursts open and the doctor comes in again.

Samford's eyes fly open. "So, did I win?" He's not sure why he is so concerned with a race that happened a month ago. At least he thinks it was a month ago. Not that he would really know. He's never been that competitive about anything before, except the number of women he can bang in a month.

"I'm afraid not," the doctor says.

"Who won?"

"No one. Don't you remember? The race was cut short. The snipers showed up. You were grazed by a bullet and collapsed on the field. It's too bad because you were winning by a lot. In fact, you were about to set a record. Does this ring a bell?" The doctor offers a smile, but it isn't the comforting type.

Samford thinks. "No. None of it. I just remember running, my balls flopping around, trying to beat the other clones."

The doctor stares at him, mouth open and brow raised. "What do you mean by the other clones?"

"It was the Clone Olympics. I had been kidnapped because I was some special clone. They trained me to win."

The doctor laughs then leans in close. "You're not a clone," he whispers.

"What the hell are you talking about? I have the serial number." He opens his mouth to try and recite the number but can't remember any of it. A string of gibberish emerges from his lips.

The doctor laughs again. "You silly humans. You have no clue. None of you."

Samford is too shocked to speak. His mouth hangs wide open, beckoning the doctor to explain.

"Let me explain," the doctor says before he begins pacing around the room, looking in drawers and underneath every visible object. It is several minutes before

119

the doctor starts explaining. Samford wonders if the doctor is checking for bugs.

"Okay, here it goes. All humans have a serial number implanted in their anuses when they are born. This has been going on since the '40s. It's the clones that don't have the serial numbers. That's the only way you can tell the difference."

"What about people born before the '40s?"

"They're too old to be cloned, so it doesn't matter."

"Why do we have serial numbers?" Samford asks, knowing the doctor will tell him anyway. He wants to look thoughtful to impress the doctor.

"It's simple, really. It's government tracking. But you probably had that figured out as soon as I told you. The government tracks everyone all the time. Everything about you. Your heart rate, how often you brush your teeth, your masturbation habits, the number of women you screw."

"Why?"

The doctor laughs again. *The laugh ends too soon for comfort, and the doctor continues.* "For control, obviously. The government is slowly gaining total control without you knowing it. Wanna hear something funny? All the politicians and all the world leaders and pretty much everyone famous: all clones."

"Why?"

"People think too much. Clones think as they are programmed."

"So who is in charge of everything? Is it a clone or a person?"

"Well, funny you should ask. The overseer of it all is –"

But the doctor's eyes roll back and he drops to the ground. The lights turn off. Samford's eyes are wide open but he can't see a thing.

Jacaranda Storm

by Kimberlee Smith

Been exactly a month to the day since Doreen appeared out of nowhere to disturb us in our little slice of nowhere, which my husband Dean and I have determined is what the living refer to as limbo, or purgatory, depending on your religious convictions. The way I grew up, there were two ways to go: up or down. Heaven or Hell. Can't say it's refreshing to have debunked that myth, but so here we are.

I'm Melodie and I died the day our daughter Etheline was born. I went by snakebite. Dean burned as if he went by way of Hell, in an explosion of fire and terror. Prop plane crashed into the tip of a mountain. Enough fuel to turn him to ash upon impact. I know because I was there, not in my body, but he didn't go down alone – he screamed until his heart gave out, thankfully right before it all blew up. But that's not the point now. Point is, this *thing*, Doreen, showed up after Dean and I were alone here for a couple months and were getting on each other's nerves, hoping for company of some sort. She wasn't company.

Tensions were rising; he was getting antsy to move on, to Heaven, maybe? In hindsight I'm not so sure that's where he's going when he moves on from this afterworld. And I've just wanted to stay here and keep an eye on our baby, watch her grow up in the care of my mum, Maybell. She's done as fine a job as can be expected. Sure, she drinks a little too much, but it's all she's got to keep her company other than the bub. She pushes Etheline in the pram every day, feeds her right, gives her a lotta love. Keeps her nappies clean, rocks her to sleep, sings her sweet songs.

So this craziness that called herself Doreen and said she had passed away and had actually been here before, but was just passing through on her way to visit her family that went before she did, was some sort of decoy ... we don't know if she was either put up to testing us or was a menacing, devious spirit trying to get us to go with her. And I don't think she was going to what is often – and misleadingly as far as my experience tells me – referred to as "a better place," she was going *down*.

It goes something like this: She tells us she knows there is more to the afterworld than where Dean and I had been lingering for the past few months; that it's futile to spend eternity just looking down on our little girl, not able to have any connection with her at all.

"That'd just break your hearts every day, and wouldn't that be the worst choice?" she asks with cloudy eyes that look like smoldering coal and smiles with a gaping mouth like a cavernous hole, darker than her eyes.

"Doesn't do that poor bub with no mum and dad no good. And it don't do nothing for you two naïve souls but make you feel bad for yourselves. That don't gain you any points in this place," says Doreen with a snort. For a split second it looks like she has a bloody nose, but then Dean freaks out, trembling so hard his vibrations shake me like an earthquake, and he secrets to me, *That's fire coming out of her nose! Like a dragon!*

Bullshit ... you sure? I volley the thought to Dean. He knows I'm begging for a different answer. But he thinks nothing to me, he just stares at Doreen and turns that rotten gray oyster color his apparition does whenever he gets out of sorts. This time it doesn't stop at that. He's like a not-any-longer human mood ring. He keeps turning until he's purple-black.

She wasn't able to read our thoughts, we believed.

"I got you and I got you two but good. You don't have any faith in this place, but I have been here before and you should take heed of my advice." Doreen is now weaving her hands throughout her midsection where she was chewed apart by a crocodile – or so she said – wildly weaving her arms in angry jerking movements, flailing and spinning.

"I ain't bleeding and it ain't fire! You don't know shit!" Doreen is screaming but her voice has dropped to a baritone and is echoing like, I don't know what else to call it but like the devil.

"No one ever said that, take it easy," I say, but then my electrical system short-circuits or goes into overdrive or whatever you want to call it when I cause the lightning and thunderstorms just by getting riled up. Doreen's been playing us all along, knowing just what we've been thinking ever since she appeared ... I don't want to say she *arrived,* because I have a feeling she's been here much longer than Dean and I, maybe forever.

"Doreen, I'm not leaving because I'm going to stay with my baby, watch her grow, at least for a while longer. There isn't anywhere better for us but here, as close as we can be to Etheline." I try to sound respectful and sincere, but with the storm all around it's not so easy.

"And enough with your fucking storms, Melodie. You think I've never seen that before? You think you're the first?" She's bleeding like a fountain now, ears, eyes, and nose. Her fists are whirring in infinity signs through what once was her midsection.

"You never been anywhere but here, you've never been on earth, you've never loved or been loved. You don't know the first thing about Heaven. You might know this place, but you don't know anything else," says Dean.

"Like Hell I don't," bellows Doreen.

The storms are going like this place is going to blow into oblivion. But then something beautifully unexpected happens. That storm quiets and then thousands of lavender jacaranda blossoms appear and whorl around Dean and me, intoxicating us in the perfume and velvet of the petals. It happens whenever there's a nostalgic loveliness in this foreign world. The phenomenon comes from – it has to – when Dean planted a garden of baby jacaranda trees for me as a surprise Christmas present, this past year right before I died. They are my favorite flowers.

Doreen stayed here and taunted us and spooked us until this morning, when she was taken against her will. We won this time. It seemed like she was sucked into a funnel, downwards, like what happens when you flush the loo. Just like Dorothy in *The Wizard of Oz*, all we had to do was believe we could go home again – to be with our bub from here, which is the best we can do – and the answer was there all along. We were being put to some sort of test. And we passed.

I'm not sure about Dean, because he'd been consumed by that rotten spirit Doreen since she presented herself to us, but more or less I've been in my own world since the day I arrived, following my mum real closely because she's always *always* with our bub. I can tell by what she's been doing recently – slowly closing up the house, overwatering the jacarandas, buying cases of throwaway nappies instead of using the ones she washes every day – that she's planning a trip. I think she's got nothing to lose, and she may well be right. I get the feeling she and Etheline are taking a car trip to find my daddy. A long drive that's long overdue. And I'm going to be there every centimeter of the way, Dean or no Dean. That's up to him.

What's Wrong with Her

by Vanessa Weibler Paris

"First was Lizzie," I start. "Really small eyes, super close together."

"I mean, how close could they possibly be?" Bobby asks, shrugging out of his jacket and tossing it on the back of his chair. It's a Christmas gift from his wife Jenny, and I wonder if the slick black leather will swallow the bar smoke. "There's a nose in the middle, right?"

"Close," I say. "And then Janie. Big gap between the front teeth."

"How big?" Bobby asks.

"Hmm," I say. "Well, Janie's front teeth were about as close to one another as Lizzie's eyes."

"Oh," says Bobby in response, and then, "oh."

"And then came Nancy," I say. I pause for a swallow of my beer. Guinness, heavy, practically a meal. It takes me a moment to force the word. "Harelip."

"Harelip?"

"I know," I say. "I didn't even know people still got those. Aren't they all fixed at birth? At least in first-world countries?"

"Poor Nancy," Bobby says, holding up his Amstel Light.

"Poor Nancy," I agree, clinking and swigging.

I almost can't believe I'm saying these things. I've spent my whole life as Slim Jim, unable to gain or maintain no matter what. I hide my body in a fog of baggy clothing and smoky bars, but I can't hide my face. Gaunt and angular, hollow-eyed and sharp-chinned. I once heard someone describe my features as "skin stretched over a skull." I feel sick speaking this way, of these women. But when you join a website called Ugly People Dating and then meet up with your best friend in the world to debrief your dates, of course he's going to ask: "What's wrong with her?"

"And then there was Maura," I tick off a finger. "Really bad skin."

"How bad could it –"

"Bad," I say. "I almost wanted to reach out and start squeezing, as if it would somehow make her feel better. Provide a release." Maura, beautiful blue eyes and a weak white smile surrounded by piles of soft red bulges. I'd wished I could free her lovely features from the spotty topography, removing them like Mr. Potato Head parts and pushing them gently onto a smooth new plastic face.

"Barbara," I tick another finger. "Facial scar, not even very big, not even that obvious. Car accident from when she was a kid. There was also Danielle," I say, adding before he asks, "who's just, you know, overweight."

Bobby coughs and busies himself with a chicken wing. He teeters on the edge of obese himself, having expanded slowly over the years. A pound this year, another the next. A stealth few ounces here and there. He would never complain about it to me, I know. He would never risk hurting me.

"Drummette?" Bobby holds out a baby drumstick, dripping with wet orange sauce. I like the drummettes; he likes the wingettes. We're not just best friends; we're each other's wingmen.

I take it gratefully, eat it skin-on. It's hot, hot enough to make my forehead sweat and nose run and throat cough. It's just right.

126

"So, the million-dollar question," Bobby says, pulling small pieces of meat free of the fat, then lining them up beside celery sticks on his plate. "Any second dates on the horizon?"

"I asked Lizzie," I admit. "She wasn't interested. But polite about it. And I called Maura. She never called back."

"Their loss," says Bobby, as I knew he would.

"But there is one," I say. And I tell him about Iris.

I tell him about Iris, whose dating profile picture was shaded, shadowed, sepiaed in silhouette. Iris, standard-sized and symmetrical featured. Iris, whose 'About Me' was left entirely blank.

I tell him about the texts swapped, the emails exchanged, the phone calls shared before we even met. About how I tried postponing the date, terrified to finally meet her, because I'd already fallen in love and didn't want it to end.

"So," Bobby says eventually, holding tight to the same celery stick he was gripping when I first began. "What's wrong with her?"

Iris had kissed me at the end of our date, my first kiss since I was a teenager at a spin-the-bottle party. She'd leaned in without any sign of revulsion, without closed eyes, and kissed me. And then she'd turned toward my ear and whispered hotly, *"I'm ugly on the inside."*

The BBQ

by Joanne Jagoda

I don't want to get up. It feels good to stay in bed. It's so quiet in this old house with the girls at their summer jobs. The graduation party was nice though not my style. Lillian pulled out all the stops as usual. Her caterer set up stations around their big yard with a sushi chef, a taco station and a bar where the kids got virgin daiquiris and pina coladas. The girls invited their friends, and I had a few teachers from school and a handful of old friends. Cassie and Robin were embarrassed that everything was so fancy but their friends got into it, playing tennis and swimming. They loved being waited on, and no one wanted to leave. I put on a good show but I was torn, missing my husband but thinking about David too. He knew about the party, but it would have been awkward to have him there. He's coming to dinner tonight to meet the girls.

Guess I better get my butt up and go to Farmer Joe's to pick up corn, tomatoes and lettuce. I'm going to grill chicken. Since Paul died I've had to learn how to barbeque. That was his specialty. I can see him in his 'Kiss the Cook' apron ... tongs in one hand and a bottle of Corona in the other. I'll stop for rolls and a cherry pie at La Tartine on Judah Street. I've got to stop picking at my cuticles. I'm nervous about tonight. What if the girls don't like him?

That's dumb. He's so sweet and asks about them all the time.

Farmer Joe's had the best organic tomatoes today. I'll wash the salad, shuck the corn and marinate the chicken in that recipe I got from *Epicurious*. I'm going to use my new paisley placemats from Cost Plus.

"Mom, I'm home."

"Hi Cass."

"Your table is very ... uh ... Martha Stewart. Nice placemats and napkins."

"I guess that's a compliment, Cass. How was the lab?"

"Extremely cool. We injected Elmo and Burt with the vaccine, and had to observe them for hours. They tolerated the treatment well for rats. Oh yeah, 'Dude' is coming tonight."

"And you can call him David, not 'Dude'."

"OK, DAY-vid. What-ev ..."

"Please try to be nice."

"Mom, I'm not a baby. I get it.""

"Robin do you have to let the door slam **every** damn time you come in?

"Ooooh ... bad language Mom ..."

"You're a pain, Rob. How was your day?"

"Not bad for babysitting a bunch of preppy brats. Oh yeah tonight we meet the 'Dude'."

"I just yelled at your sister about that. His name is *David*. And do I have to remind you to be civil too? And don't spoil your dinner with ice cream."

"Chill Mom. We're not six. Come on, Cass. Let's go upstairs."

"I'm going up to shower." Just a dab of this perfume he likes. And these high-heeled sandals are cute. I look acceptable ... oh hell, I look good. It's been a long time since I've felt this way. David has been hinting about taking a long weekend in the Napa Valley. I get all tingly just thinking about it.

"I'm starting the grill and you two get out of your jeans. I'll put on the chicken in ten minutes."

"We HEAR you Mom!" Robin yells down to the yard.

I'm going to sit in the car a minute. This is my big night. I've been waiting to meet the twins. Just one more step to getting closer to the family. These gifts I selected for them should do the trick.

Oh, there's the door. He's right on time. He looks cute in his jeans and a yellow polo shirt, and his hair is all messy from the convertible. I feel like I'm sixteen.

"Annie, you look delicious and your perfume ... is mmmm. Here, these are for you."

"Oh, these wildflowers are gorgeous, thank you ... and you brought wine too." He is holding two small blue boxes. I think they are from Tiffany's. Paul splurged on a Tiffany ring for our twentieth anniversary. "Girls, come meet David."

"David Lewis, meet my daughters. Cassie and Robin meet David." *Why are they so quiet. They usually don't shut up.*

"Hello young ladies. These are graduation presents for you. Go ahead ... open them."

I know they don't recognize the Tiffany boxes. I hope they like what he got them. Ah, Cassie got a silver bangle and Robin's is a silver heart pendant. Why don't they thank him? Damn it girls, say something. Where are your manners?

Robin finally pipes up, "Uh thank you Du ... ah David. It's, uh pretty."

"Yeah, thanks, David. Come on Rob. Let's try them on upstairs."

"Girls, we're having a glass of wine on the patio. Dinner in thirty."

"OK, Mom."

"David, let's sit outside. San Francisco doesn't get many warm nights. Thank you for the gifts, from Tiffany's no less. How did you know what they'd like? Half the time I get them the wrong thing."

"I'll let you in on my secret. My sister in London has teenagers and they tell me what they like to get for their birthdays and Christmas."

She's so easy to fool. My sister hates my guts and doesn't have children. It was so easy to hack the twins' computers and see the search engines they look at.

Oh my god, he's turning the chicken just like Paul. I better have some wine or I'll lose it.

"David, I like this wine."

"It's a Mondavi Chardonnay. We'll go to their winery in the Napa Valley. Have you picked our weekend?"

Cassie and Robin huddle in their bedroom. "He's cute, Rob and don't you love his accent? Mom is gaga over him, and he's trying hard to get on our good side."

"Yeah, he's cute, but I get a creepy vibe from him."

"You've hardly said two words to him."

"How did he pick the perfect gifts for us? I was just looking at something like that online."

"Rob, it's a nice coincidence. Don't you believe in coincidences?"

"Girls!!"

"Anne, dinner was delicious. I never knew you were such a good cook. Girls, tell me about your summer jobs. Cassie, I heard you work in a lab."

"Actually David, we'd like to know about you," Robin interrupts before Cassie can answer.

"Well Robin, I'm from London and came to open a new branch office and —"

"But what does your company do?"

Anne forces a laugh. "Rob, don't bug David. Let's have dessert. I bought the best cherry pie."

Robin glares at her mother but stops asking questions while they eat dessert.

"Another slice David?"

"Uh, no," he pats his stomach and takes Anne's hand. "Cassie and Robin, I hope you won't mind me taking your mom on a getaway to the Napa Valley next month."

Robin's eyes grow wide. She stands up so fast her chair falls backward. "Mom, how could you?" Robin stomps out and Cassie follows her.

Anne shrugs and stammers, "You have to give them time David. You're the first man I've brought home since their father died."

David tries to grin and yanks Anne up from her chair. He whispers in a low voice, "I want to be with you. They'll have to get used it." She shivers when he nuzzles her neck.

"Well … let's try for … uh, late July. Maybe it's better during the week rather than the weekend if you can take off. That way I can spend the weekend with them."

"Sure, whatever you want."

That little bitch, Robin. I knew she'd be trouble. Now I have to re-arrange everything.

He looks at his iPhone. "How about Wednesday July 30th? We'll start off early and stay a couple nights. You'd be back on Friday."

"That'll work."

"We'll tour wineries, have gourmet meals, go for mud baths and leave plenty of time for uh … well, you know …"

Anne blushes and kisses him. He kisses her back hard.

"I'm heading out, Anne. Look … I really want this trip to happen. And thank you for dinner."

"I'll speak to them. They'll be OK with it." She closes the door after him and sighs.

I hope he isn't mad. He has to give them some time. Shit. He did seem a little put out.

"Mom, I'll help you with the dishes. Rob is upstairs pouting. David's cute and all, but he sure surprised us."

Robin bursts in and blurts out. "He's weird. There's something about him. How did he know to pick that particular jewelry? We had just been looking at those."

"Robin, he's got teenage nieces and good taste. Nothing wrong with that. I get it that he'll never be your dad, but I have fun with him. It was rude the way you left the table."

"I don't like him. Anyway, we're meeting Laurie and Kate at the Metreon."

The door slams.

Why can't they give him a chance? They wanted me to date. I'm so damn frustrated. I'm going to mop the kitchen floor.

I don't want to clean the damn floor. I'm going to have another glass of wine. I knew things were going too perfectly.

Authors

Rachel Ambrose is a twenty-something fiction writer from Connecticut. Her favorite season is winter, she enjoys well-made Manhattans, and she loves Southern fiction. Her work has appeared in *Crack the Spine*, *Exiles Literary Magazine*, and *The Colton Review*. Currently at work on her second novel, she blogs at http://victorywhiskeyjuliet.tumblr.com.

Lynn Beighley is a fiction writer stuck in a technical book writer's body. Her stories often involve deeply flawed characters and the unsatisfying meshing of the virtual and actual world. She has an MFA in Creative Writing and currently has 16 books published.

Margaret Bingel is just a writer, living in Manchester, New Hampshire. She spends her time working at her father's beer store, art modeling, and writing (when she can). She doesn't have a website or a blog yet, but who knows, maybe she'll have one in the future.

Guilie Castillo-Oriard is a Mexican writer currently exiled on the island of Curaçao. She misses Mexican food and Mexican *amabilidad*, but the laissez-faire attitude and the beaches of the Caribbean are fair exchange. Plus, the bounty of cultural diversity inspires great culture-clash fiction. Guilie is currently revising and editing her first novel. Her short stories have appeared in *Fiction 365*, *Lady Ink Magazine* and *Pure Slush*. She blogs at http://guilie-castillo-oriard.blogspot.com.

John Wentworth Chapin lives and writes in Baltimore, where he is too frequently starting Project B before finishing Project A. John writes non-fiction as well as fiction. Find him on the web at http://johnwentworthchapin.com.

James Claffey hails from County Westmeath, Ireland, and lives on an avocado ranch in Carpinteria, CA with his family. He is the author of a collection of short fiction, *Blood a Cold Blue*. His website can be found at http://jamesclaffey.com.

Gay Degani has published online and in print including *The Best of Every Day Fiction* editions and her own collection, *Pomegranate Stories*. She is the founder-editor emeritus of EDF's *Flash Fiction Chronicles*, a staff editor at *Smokelong Quarterly*, and blogs at *Words in Place* where a list of her work can be found. She's had two stories nominated for Pushcart consideration and won the eleventh Annual Glass Woman Prize for her flash piece, *Something about L.A.*

Michelle Elvy is an editor and writer who has meandered from the shores of the Chesapeake to New Zealand's Bay of Islands. Michelle has published poetry, short stories and non-fiction about travel, faraway places, food, motorcycling, slow travel, the kindness of strangers and raising children in unusual places for numerous literary journals and magazines in the US, Canada, Australasia, UK and Europe. She edits at *Flash Frontier: An Adventure in Short Fiction* and *Blue Five Notebook*. She can also be found regularly at *Awkword Paper Cut*. More about manuscript assessment and Michelle's take on editing and writing at http://michelleelvy.com.

Gloria Garfunkel is the daughter of two Auschwitz survivors which deeply affected her whole life and personality. She has a Ph.D. from Harvard University in Psychology and Social Relations, concentrating on Personality Development Studies. She was a psychotherapist for thirty years working with children, adults and families. She is currently retired, reading and writing to her heart's content. She has published many stories in journals and anthologies and hopes to eventually publish a collection of her flash fiction. Find more at her blog http://queruloussquirreldaily.blogspot.com/

Teresa Burns Gunther has had fiction and nonfiction appear in numerous literary journals and most recently in *Northwind Magazine*, *Bookslut* and *Best New Writing 2012*. Teresa is the Editor of *The Lakeside*, an on-line literary magazine, and she founded Lakeshore Writers Workshop in Oakland, California where she leads creative writing workshops and classes and works one-on-one with writers. You can find more of her work at her website http://www.teresaburnsgunther.com/.

Gill Hoffs lives with her family and an ever-dwindling supply of Nutella in the North of England. Find Gill on facebook or as @gillhoffs on twitter, email her a dirty joke at gillhoffs@hotmail.co.uk, or leave a clean comment at http://gillhoffs.wordpress.com/. *Wild: a collection* is out now from *Pure Slush Books*. Her non-fiction book *The Sinking of RMS Tayleur: the Lost Story of the Victorian Titanic* is also out now from *Pen & Sword*. (See her site or http://www.pen-and-sword.co.uk/ for details.) Feel free to send her chocolate.

Joanne Jagoda of Oakland, California, took an inspiring writing workshop after retiring in 2009, and launched on a long-postponed creative writing journey. Since discovering her passion for writing, she has worked non-stop on short stories, poetry and non-fiction. Her work has appeared in a number of e-zines and print anthologies, including *Pure Slush* and *Idea Gems Magazine*, and she was a poet of the month for a Jewish news weekly in Northern California. When not taking writing and poetry classes, Joanne enjoys being a writer-coach for ninth graders, Zumba, and visiting her three grandchildren in Jerusalem.

Len Kuntz is a writer from Washington State and an editor at the online literary magazine *Metazen*. His work appears widely in print and online, and you can find more of his work at http://lenkuntz.blogspot.com.

Sally-Anne Macomber was born and raised in Toronto, Canada, and studied journalism at Concordia University in Montreal. Her work on high fashion and the demise of haute couture has appeared in various online and print publications in both Europe and North America. She turned to writing flash fiction in 2010, and hasn't looked back.

Jessica McHugh is an author of speculative fiction that spans the genre from horror and alternate history to epic fantasy. A member of the Horror Writers Association and a 2013 Pulp Ark nominee, she has devoted herself to novels, short stories, poetry, and playwriting. Jessica has had thirteen books published in five years, including the bestselling *Rabbits in the Garden*, *The Sky: The World* and the gritty coming-of-age thriller, *PINS*. More info on her speculations and publications can be found at http://www.jessicamchughbooks.com.

Gwendolyn Joyce Mintz is a fiction writer and aspiring photographer. Her work has appeared in various online and print publications. In other incarnations, Mintz is a writing instructor, a teddy bear maker and somebody's grandmother.

Mandy Nicol grew up in Melbourne, Australia, and made a tree change to country Victoria in the mid-nineties – the decade, not her age. She has various animals including a flockette of pet sheep that are thankful for her vegaquarian habits. She writes short stories and loves flash fiction. *Pure Slush* is the first venue to publish her work.

Derek Osborne lives in eastern Pennsylvania. His work has appeared in *Boston Literary Magazine, Bartleby Snopes, Literary Orphans, The Linnet's Wings, Pure Slush* and many others. To read more visit http://gertrudesflat.blogspot.com, or email him at derekosborne1@gmail.com.

Vanessa Weibler Paris lives in Erie, Pa., with a guy, a girl, a boy, a bunny rabbit and a dog. She writes things both real (for work) and pretend (for fun). Her favorite things include hot peppers, bad puns, small-world stories, and tales with a twist at the end.

Gary Percesepe is Associate Editor at *New World Writing* (formerly *Mississippi Review*) and a Contributor at *The Nervous Breakdown*. Author of four books in philosophy, Percesepe's poetry, fiction, essays, and interviews have appeared in *Story Quarterly, N + 1, Salon, Mississippi Review, The Millions, Brevity, PANK, Metazen, The Brooklyner*, and other places. His collection of short stories, *Why I Did the Grocery Girl*, is forthcoming from *Aqueous Books*. He has taught at Saint Louis University, Wittenberg University, and University of Dayton. He lives in Buffalo, New York.

Matt Potter is an Australian-born writer who keeps a part of his psyche in Berlin. Matt has been published in various places online, and he is, rather amazingly, also the founding editor of *Pure Slush*. You can find more of his work at his website: http://mattcpotter.webs.com/.

Darryl Price was born in Kentucky and educated at Thomas More College. A founding member of L. Jack Roth's Yellow Pages Poets, he has published dozens of chapbooks, and his poems have appeared in many journals. He currently edits *Olentangy Review* with his wife Melissa.

Stephen V. Ramey is an American author from New Castle, Pennsylvania. His work has appeared in many places, including *The Doctor TJ Eckleburg Review*, *The Journal of Compressed Creative Arts*, and *A Capella Zoo*. *Glass Animals*, his first collection of (very) short fiction is available from *Pure Slush Books*. Find him and more of his work at http://www.stephenvramey.com.

Shane Simmons is a self-confessed coffee shop writer who believes that regardless of quality, each paragraph penned should be rewarded with sweet treats (cake, muffins, Belgian waffles, etc). London-born, he ran away to Glasgow ten years ago, expanded his waistline and now blogs at http://scribblingsimmons.wordpress.com/.

Kimberlee Smith is a writer whose poetry, essays, fiction, and creative non-fiction have been published in numerous literary journals and anthologies. She was awarded a residency to the Jentel Arts Program in 2013. She lives with her two daughters, two dogs, three cats, two rabbits, and nine chooks on her farm in rural Connecticut. She received her MA in English from the University of Sydney, a certificate in the Creative Writing Program through UCLA, and her BA in Journalism from the University of Southern

California. She is enrolled currently in post-graduate studies at Columbia University in New York. She can do a headstand on a trampoline, kill a chook, and make hard cider from the apples in her orchard.

Andrew Stancek was born in Bratislava and saw Russian tanks occupying his homeland. His dreams of circuses and ice cream, flying and lion-taming, miracle and romance have appeared recently in print in *LA Review*, *Windsor Review* and *New Sun Rising: Stories for Japan*. Among the many online publications featuring his work are *Every Day Fiction*, *Gemini Magazine* (Flash Fiction Contest Grand Prize Winner), *fwriction*, *r.kv.r.y. quarterly literary journal*, *Tin House*, *Flash Fiction* Chronicles, *The Linnet's Wings*, *Connotation Press*, *THIS Literary Magazine*, *LA Review*, *Windsor Review*, *Thrice Fiction Magazine*, *New Sun Rising*, and *Pure Slush* online.

Susan Tepper is the author of four published books of fiction and a chapbook of poetry. Her most recent title *The Merrill Diaries* (*Pure Slush Books*, July 2013) is a Novel in Stories that follows a young woman's adventures in love and lust on two continents, spanning a decade. Tepper has received nine Pushcart nominations, and one for the Pulitzer Prize in fiction. You can visit her website here: http://www.susantepper.com.

Nathaniel Tower lives in the Twin Cities with his wife and daughter. After teaching high school English for nine years, he decided to pursue a career in writing / publishing / editing. His fiction has appeared in over two hundred online and print journals. His first collection of fiction, *Nagging Wives, Foolish Husbands*, was released in 2014 through *Martian Lit*. Nathaniel is the founding and managing editor of *Bartleby Snopes Literary Magazine and Press*. You can find out more about Nathaniel at http://nathanieltower.wordpress.com.

Townsend Walker lives in San Francisco. His stories have been published in over fifty literary journals and included in seven anthologies. One story won the SLO NightWriters story contest. Two were nominated for the PEN / O. Henry Award. Four were performed at the New Short Fiction Series in Hollywood. He is associate editor at *Grey Sparrow Journal*. During a career in finance he published three books, on foreign exchange, derivatives and portfolio management. Educated at Georgetown, NYU and Stanford, his website is at http://www.townsendwalker.com.

Michael Webb is continually surprised anyone is interested in what he has to say, and he blogs occasionally at http://innocentsaccidentshints.blogspot.com.

Other volumes in the *2014* series from Pure Slush

Visit the Pure Slush Store:
http://pureslush.webs.com/store.htm

January 2014 Vol. 1
ISBN: 978-1-925101-03-4

February 2014 Vol. 2
ISBN: 978-1-925101-14-0

March 2014 Vol. 3
ISBN: 978-1-925101-17-1

April 2014 Vol. 4
ISBN: 978-1-925101-27-0

May 2014 Vol. 5
ISBN: 978-1-925101-30-0

July 2014 Vol. 7
ISBN: 978-1-925101-37-9

www.ingramcontent.com/pod-product-compliance
Lightning Source LLC
Chambersburg PA
CBHW050757250626
47155CB00005B/2103